ABOUT THE C

An erotica-writing dominatri ⏤ ⏤wning French-man. A priest who leads a double life. Together, they are the Unholy Trinity—the unconventional trio at the heart of *USA Today* bestseller Tiffany Reisz's Original Sinners series.

This sampler contains excerpts from several of the most popular Original Sinners titles, as well as the complete text of the long out-of-print short story, "The Teacher's Pet."

Reisz's erotic romance series spans nine full-length novels, over a dozen novellas, and countless short stories—over a million words in all to date. Before you dive in, however, remember: *No safe word can protect the heart....*

"Daring, sophisticated, and literary... Exactly what good erotica should be." — **Kitty Thomas on *The Siren***

"Stunning... Transcends genres and will leave readers abso-lutely breathless." — *RT Book Reviews* **on the Original Sinners series**

"I worship at the altar of Tiffany Reisz!" — *New York Times* **bestselling author Lorelei James**

THE ORIGINAL SINNERS SERIES

TIFFANY REISZ

THE ORIGINAL SINNERS

8TH CIRCLE PRESS
LOUISVILLE, KY

Trade Paperback ISBN: 978-1-949769-44-9

Also available as an ebook

Cover design by Andrew Shaffer

Front cover image(s) used under license from Shutterstock.com

www.8thcirclepress.com

First Edition

CONTENTS

A WHISKEY CHASER

EXCERPT FROM "THE SIREN," THE FIRST
BOOK IN THE ORIGINAL SINNERS SERIES

Notorious Nora Sutherlin is famous for her delicious works of erotica, each one more popular with readers than the last. But her latest manuscript is different—more serious, more personal—and she's sure it'll be her breakout book...if it ever sees the light of day.

Zachary Easton holds Nora's fate in his well-manicured hands. The demanding British editor agrees to handle the book on one condition: he wants complete control. Nora must rewrite the entire novel to his exacting standards—in six weeks—or it's no deal.

Nora's grueling writing sessions with Zach are draining...and shockingly arousing. And a dangerous former lover has her wondering which is more torturous—staying away from him...or returning to his bed?

Nora thought she knew everything about being pushed to your limits. But in a world where passion is pain, nothing is ever that simple.

THE
SIREN

S tanding, Zach reached for the bottle, but Nora beat him to it. She held it in her hand and gave him the most dangerous smile he'd ever seen.

"Zach…let's play a game."

It took five minutes before Zach regretted coming to Nora's.

"Truth or drink?" Zach asked as he shed his coat. "You will recall I'm in my forties."

"There's no age limit on alcohol-induced stupidity," Nora countered. "And this is an easy game. I ask a question and either you answer it or you take a shot. Same rules for me. Whoever gets the drunkest loses, or wins, depending on your mood."

"This game is hardly fair. You are far more forthcoming than any other person I've ever met." Zach tossed his coat over the back of Nora's armchair.

Nora leaned forward across her desk.

"Trust me, Easton. You've got secrets you want to keep. I've got secrets I have to keep. I think we're pretty evenly matched here."

"Is that so?" he asked, his curiosity piqued. "Let's find out then."

"Game on," Nora said. "You go first."

Zach knew his first question immediately. "I'll ask you the question you didn't answer today—who is, excuse me, was Ellie?"

"Ellie was me once upon a time. My mother and friends always called me Elle or Ellie. Søren, being rather formal, calls me Eleanor. I was born Eleanor Schreiber."

"A German Catholic then. This poor Jew is even more intimidated. So Nora Sutherlin is your pen name?"

"It's the name I work under, yes," she said, and Zach thought he saw a shadow of one of her secrets cross her face.

"But that's two questions. My turn—why did your wife leave you? Or was it you who left her?"

Zach leaned forward, poured his whiskey and took a shot. He swallowed a cough as the liquor burned his throat and stomach all the way down. He hadn't done any hard drinking in a long time. He was afraid if he started he would never stop. Here with Nora he still felt as if he was at a funeral but now at least it was a jazz funeral.

"Fair enough," Nora said. "Your turn."

"On the subject of our respective exes, why did you leave your mysterious and formal Søren?"

Nora seemed to think about it. She reached forward, poured her shot and downed it.

"Søren's off-limits," she said. "More for his sake than mine. My turn to ask—are you going to sign my contract?"

"Honest answer, I don't know." Zach worried Nora would be hurt by his reticence. "It's going well, better than I'd hoped. But there's still a great deal of work to do on it. And I never know if I like a book until I've read the last page. The ending makes or breaks every book. I hope that doesn't upset you."

"Water off a drunk's back." Nora raised her shot glass to him in a salute. "Your turn."

"Why is Søren such a secret?"

Nora smirked at him and downed her whiskey without the hint of a cough or discomfort.

"You're trying to get me drunk. I appreciate that. I will tell you this—I highly doubt Søren is a secret for the same reason your wife, ex-wife, whatever, is."

"Who is also off-limits."

"Let's forget wives then. How about lovers? Ever had a threesome?"

"There's no warm-up here, is it? It's just straight for the jugular."

"I'm known for my directness, gorgeous. Answer or drink."

"The answer," Zach said, "is that I'm going to drink."

Nora hooted with laughter.

"I'll take that as a yes then," she said as Zach swallowed hard and set his shot glass down with an emphatic clink.

"It is a yes, but I wanted the whiskey anyway."

"My kind of guy. Who, what, where, when, and can you draw me a picture?"

Zach leaned back in the armchair and felt the heat from the drink and the memory quickly rushing to his head.

"I will admit I barely remember the evening. It was when I was at university, as a student not a professor, and I was at a birthday party. I believe there was some Irish whiskey involved in that night, as well. I was seeing a young lady, and her rather liberated flatmate decided to join us in bed after the party. Lovely girls, both of them. One's married to an M.P. now."

"I'm jealous," she said. She left her chair and crawled up onto her desk and sat on top of it cross-legged. "I've never had a threesome with two other women. All of mine have been with one man and one woman. Or two men." She looked down at him and winked.

"Can't believe there's anything you haven't done. Is there anything else?"

"One or two things. Keep asking, you might find out what they are."

Zach knew she expected a question about her sex life. He decided to try a different approach.

"Apart from the occasional heroic rescue you don't really seem to need the services of a live-in personal assistant. Why did you ask Wesley to move in?"

Nora blinked and reached for her shot. Her hand pulled back and she met Zach's eyes.

"Wesley… That kid blew my mind from day one. He was so damn sweet. I'm not around sweet people very often. When I had him in class I found myself doing something I hadn't done in a long time."

"What was that?"

"Smiling. I'd been working so much, living a pretty hard life. Wes was the opposite of me in so many ways—soft where I was hard. Probably hard where I'm soft, too." She laughed again. "He made me feel human again…like the kind of person who could stay up too late watching stupid movies and talking. I'd forgotten how to be normal, or maybe I never knew how. My life got weird at a pretty young age and it's been weird ever since. But Wes came along and suddenly I had another reason to get out of bed in the morning besides money."

"Are you in love with him?" Zach asked.

"That's two questions," Nora said, wagging a finger at him. She downed her shot. "That wasn't me admitting to being in love with the kid. That was me being driven to drink yet again by that twerp."

"Frustrating roommate, I imagine."

"Very. No one that sexy should be that off-limits. I could say the same about you."

"I'm your editor, Nora. I don't think we should be involved," Zach said, squirming a little in his seat. "J.P. would kill us both."

"You're not scared of J.P. and we both know it. It's me you're scared of—why?"

Zach gave the question some thought. The three shots had gone quickly to his head on his empty stomach. He felt lightheaded and warm. He knew Nora deserved an answer no matter how badly he didn't want to tell her.

He picked up his shot glass.

"Again, I'll answer. But not without some liquid fortification," he said and took his drink. He bent over for a moment and breathed. He looked up and saw Nora looking down at him, waiting patiently. "You're beautiful enough and wild enough that you make me think things I never thought I would think again and feel things I didn't think I'd ever feel again. And you make me afraid I'll start forgetting things I don't ever want to forget. You're dangerous."

She nodded her head and didn't look flattered.

"You're not the first man who's called me that. When I was sixteen, Søren told me that there were suicide bombers on the Gaza Strip who were less dangerous than I was."

"I thought Søren was off-limits for discussion."

"He was. But I'm getting drunk fast and have very little self-control under the best of circumstances. You could get Søren ten times as shit-faced as we're getting and he'd still have the self-control of a desert father."

"He must not be that disciplined if he made love to you at such a young age."

"Young age? That bastard made me wait until I was twenty years old, Zach. You are sitting in the office of probably the most famous erotica writer since Anaïs Nin and she's telling you that she didn't lose her virginity until she was twenty," Nora said and shook her head.

"I'm aghast. Why so long?"

"If he just wanted sex he would have taken me on day one, I have no doubt. But with D/s couples, the sex is the least of it. He wanted obedience, total submission. Keeping me a virgin waiting for him for so long proved he owned me even more than fucking me would have. He was also preparing me for everything he had planned. S&M is not for children or the faint of heart. He had to wait to make sure I was neither. My question now—how old were you?"

Zach stared at her. She reached out and he handed her his shot glass. She refilled it and handed it back.

"Younger than twenty," he said and raised his glass to drink.

Nora cleared her throat and waved her hand in a "give it up" gesture. Zach put his glass down.

"Oh, very well, I was thirteen," Zach said and had a sudden memory of running off into the trees behind his school with his best mate's pretty older sister and coming out ten minutes later with a smile on his face.

"Holy shit," Nora said, laughing. "Good thing Wes is watching those middle school kids tonight."

"She was only fourteen and while it was a rather awkward and quick affair, it was hardly traumatizing or particularly scandalous."

"My first time was orchestrated and took all night, and I could barely move for a week after. I guess since I put Søren back up for discussion, we can talk about your wife."

"Not drunk enough for that."

"Well, keep drinking and at least tell me why it's so hard for you to talk about her."

While they'd been talking, the sun had set. Zach sipped at his whiskey while Nora flipped on her desk lamp. Warm light suffused the dark room and cast amber shadows everywhere he looked. Turning his head, Zach saw his reflection in the window. But he didn't see himself. He saw the door behind him and the door opened and in the doorway stood Grace who should have been anywhere in the world but standing in his doorway…

"Talking about how it ended, why it ended…it feels too much like it ended. And I don't know if I'm ready for that, Nora. I'm sorry."

"I understand not wanting something to be over. Can you at least tell me how it began?"

Zach tapped his knee with his half-empty shot glass.

"It began very badly. I would say we were doomed from the start."

Nora slid off her desk and sank to the floor in front of him. He thought it looked like an excellent idea. He joined her on the floor and leaned back against the chair.

He watched Nora take down the whiskey bottle and pour another shot.

"That year after I left Søren, I became obsessed with one question—when was it, when were we, irrevocable? When did all the little tumblers fall into place and our fate was locked in and it became impossible for us to be anything other than what we became? When was the guilty moment?"

"Did you find your answer?"

Nora shook her head. "Never. I suppose doom and destiny are just two sides of the same coin."

"I don't have to ask or wonder. I know my guilty moment. But you left your lover and mine left me. You could go back to yours, couldn't you?"

"Zach, Søren isn't some boyfriend you have a fight with and then kiss and make up. He's the invading army you surrender to before it burns your village down."

"He sounds even more dangerous than you are."

"He is. By far. He's also the best man I've ever known. Tell me about Grace. What's she like?"

Zach paused before answering. How could he describe his wife to anyone? To him Grace was the open arms he fell into when he crawled into bed at 2:00 a.m. after staying up reading a new manuscript. She was the laughing water thief in the shower at least one morning a week. She was the quiet comfort and the hand he'd been unable to let go of at his mother's funeral three years ago. Unable to get the words past his throat, Grace had taken his notes from his hand and read his eulogy for him. She was every evening and every morning and every night, and during the day when they were apart he was always happy knowing evening and night and morning were coming again.

"Grace is…well-named. She's intelligent, far smarter than I. A poet and a schoolteacher," Zach said as the alcohol swirled around his head. "She has red hair and the most perfect freckles I've ever seen on a woman." Zach closed his eyes. The first time he'd seen her completely naked when they'd made love in his bed the first time, he'd almost stopped breathing. "Even on her back all the way to her hips…the most perfect dusting of freckles."

"Freckles? That's just ruthless, isn't it?"

"Merciless. No woman that beautiful should also have freckles." Zach laughed mirthlessly. "She would lie across my lap in the evenings and read her obscure Welsh poets while I worked on a manuscript. Once she fell asleep on my lap. I used my red pen to connect all the freckles on her lower back. She was livid. We laughed for days about it."

"You had a good marriage. What happened?"

Zach stared at Nora. She sat two feet away from him but it seemed an ocean of truth and lies and memories lay between them. He held out his shot glass. She refilled it with a shaky hand. Zach drank the whiskey and enjoyed the burn all the way down.

"This is a terrible game." He closed his eyes and leaned back against the chair.

"I know a better one."

Something in Nora's voice sobered him up momentarily. He opened his eyes and Nora now sat even closer to him. She had something behind her back.

Zach reached out and brushed her cheek with the back of his hand. He raised his hand to her hair, pulled the ink pens out and watched the dark curls fall around her face.

"How long has it been?" Nora asked, her voice soft and insinuating.

"Thirteen months." He didn't have to ask what Nora meant by her question. He didn't have to think before he answered it.

"How long's it been for Grace?"

Zach took a hard breath.

"Less than thirteen months. Friday…she emailed me. Bill questions, addresses, all sorts of marital flotsam. She casually mentioned some bloke named Ian."

Nora winced.

"How casually?"

"Not casually enough for me to not picture them in bed together. It's my own fault. When we decided there was a chance our marriage was going to work—we made each other promise no secrets and no lies. I told her I could get over anything, even straying, as long as she didn't lie to me about it. I hate lying more than anything." Zach shook his head. "Here we are eight months separated and she still can't lie to me about anything, damn that girl."

Zach looked at Nora and saw something flash across her eyes, some secret worry of her own.

"I'm sorry," Nora said and Zach could tell she meant it. Zach ran a single finger over Nora's forehead and down her face. With his thumb he caressed her full bottom lip.

"Thank you. So what's the new game? This one's about to drive me to quit drinking."

"Perish the thought. Ever played 'I've never'?"

"I've never played I've never." Zach knew he was as drunk now as he'd been in a long time.

"Fun game. Very easy. I say something I've never done, and if you've actually done it then you take a shot."

"What haven't you done?"

"A few things. For example, I've never…" She leaned in toward him. She moved close enough he could smell her perfume and even taste it on his burning tongue, close enough to feel the heat radiating from her body. "I've never let an erotica writer handcuff me to her desk and go down on me."

Something caught in Zach's throat. He looked into Nora's eyes and felt the foundations of his resolve shudder. He'd never let a woman handcuff him and do anything to him. But tonight…he looked down at his shot glass.

"Never done that. Never will."

"You sure about that?" Nora stared him down. He reached out to touch her knee, and she slapped the handcuffs on his right wrist. "Look familiar? I thought we should put your prankster's gift to good use at least once."

"You're out of your mind."

"And you're so turned on right now you can hardly breathe. Your pupils are dilated, your skin is flushed, and it's not from the whiskey and we both know it."

Zach met her eyes and said nothing.

"Thirteen months, Zach. You don't need to be afraid of me anymore."

He had a vague memory of standing on Nora's porch thinking that if he crossed her threshold tonight for any reason other than her book everything would change between them. Zach took the shot glass in his hand. He looked down at the amber liquid and then back into Nora's eyes. Raising the glass to his lips, he downed his shot. He watched a grin spread ear to ear across Nora's face. For a single moment she was all smiles.

"Good boy."

For someone he thought was as drunk as he, Nora moved with a swiftness and precision that almost terrified him. She pushed him on his back, yanked his arms over his head and cuffed his wrists around the leg of her desk. Straddling him at the stomach, Nora unbuttoned her black silk pajama top and let it slide off her arms. He felt the wisp of silk brush his face before she threw it aside and on top of his coat. Under her shirt she wore a black bra that revealed far more than it concealed. He couldn't take his eyes off her curves, off her pale skin and shoulders.

Nora slid her hands under his T-shirt. Her hands on his bare skin sent every nerve firing. She bent over and kissed the center of his stomach. Unzipping his jeans, she worked them down low enough to expose the top of his hips. Zach inhaled sharply when she bit his hip bone.

"Nora—"

Nora rose up and covered his lips with one finger.

"Søren used to call me his Siren," she whispered, bending over him until she hovered an inch away from his face. "He said the things I did with my mouth could blow any man off course. Don't you want to know what he meant by that?"

Zach didn't answer but Nora didn't seem to care. She started at his neck and kissed her way down his body. A soft sigh escaped his lips as she took him in her mouth. Not even all that alcohol could blunt the pleasure of what her tongue, her lips did to him. Her hair covered her face like a veil. The tendrils of her curls tickled his stomach.

So long…it had been so long since he'd felt something so intense, so sharp that he could almost mistake the pleasure for pain. Zach ached to touch Nora but when he tried he remembered the handcuffs.

"Relax, Zach. Just enjoy." Nora paused to kiss his stomach again. "Your only job right now is to surrender."

Surrender? He'd forgotten how. He took a deep breath and laid his head back as she kept working on him. Pressure built deep in his hips.

"Nora," he gasped a warning that she didn't heed. He flinched hard and came with a ragged breath. Through the haze of alcohol and orgasm he saw Nora sit up on his thighs.

She picked up the whiskey, poured it and downed him and the shot in one swallow.

She looked down at him.

"I love a whiskey chaser."

———

THE STORY CONTINUES in The Siren, *available now in trade paperback, ebook, and audio from Harlequin's Mira Books and Mills & Boon.*

PLAYING WITH POLLY

EXCERPT FROM "THE CHATEAU," THE FIRST BOOK IN THE CHATEAU SPIN-OFF SERIES

As the Jack-of-All-Wicked-Trades for a secretive French military intelligence agency, Lieutenant Kingsley Boissonneault has done it all—spied, lied, and killed under orders. But his latest assignment is quite out of the ordinary. His commanding officer's nephew has disappeared inside a sex cult, and Kingsley has been tasked with bringing him home to safety.

The cult's holy book is Story of O, *the infamous French novel of extreme sadomasochism. Their château is a looking-glass world where women reign and men are their willing slaves. Or are they willing? It's Kingsley's mission to find out.*

Once inside the château, however, Kingsley quickly falls under the erotic spell cast by the enigmatic Madame, a woman of wisdom, power, and beauty. She offers Kingsley the one thing he's always wanted. But the price? Giving up forever the only person he's ever loved.

The ropes around his wrists were long enough Polly didn't have to untie him. Kingsley simply rolled onto his stomach and moved back into place, the ropes twisting into a knot. The pressure on his wrists was comfortable, but tight enough to feel like a pair of strong hands. Strong hands on his wrists, Kingsley lying prone, someone about to take him…

Just like high school.

"I see you smiling," Polly said as she moved off the bed to do whatever it was she needed to do.

"Just remembering," he said. "It's funny. I don't usually smile when I remember…"

"What?"

"Anything."

Polly kissed the back of his shoulder. "I'll give you a memory to make you smile."

Kingsley let out a breath of pleasure as Polly laid her hand flat on the small of his back and caressed him there.

"This is my favorite part," she said.

"Back rubs?"

"No, silly boy. Backs are my favorite part. Boy backs. My favorite body part," she said. "Right here." With her fingertips she lightly scored the center of his back where his tailbone met his spine. "Maybe that's why I love doing this so much. The view of you is divine…"

With a compliment like that, how could Kingsley object to anything she wanted to do with his body? Polly whispered instructions in his ear. He did as told, and he did it with pleasure. He pulled his knees up under him and spread them. Polly worked the plug out of him carefully.

She positioned herself behind him and started to slowly… slowly…slowly enter him. Too slowly.

Polly told him to lay flat, to stretch out his legs—however was most comfortable for him. He was under the strictest of orders to tell her the second he felt a moment's pain. But there was no pain, no discomfort. Fullness, yes. Not pain. Not like he'd known once.

"You like this, don't you?" Polly said as she kissed and licked the back of his neck. "Being taken? Penetrated? Used?"

"Very much."

"Say it then," she said.

"Say what?"

"Say you like penetration. You said you aren't shy, so say it. Or are you shy?"

He opened his mouth, laughed softly. "You make me feel shy. It's an accomplishment."

"Kingsley…" Polly said as she nibbled on his earlobe. "Say it or I'll stop fucking you…" Her voice was teasing, but the order was an order. It had to be obeyed.

"I like being penetrated," he said. "There. Happy?"

"So very happy. If I keep doing this," she said and thrust into him, "will you come?"

"Yes."

"You're sure?"

"I would bet my life on it."

"You've come from penetration alone before?"

"I have."

"High school?"

"Wouldn't you like to know?"

Polly, of course, pinched him for not answering. Pinched him and fucked him a little harder. Her thrusts into him were firm and steady, purposeful but not too hard, deep but not too deep. Every retreat wrenched a moan from his lips and every return thrust sent him panting. The inflexible object inside him stroked neglected nerves with every pass, massaging deep muscles with every welcome invasion. Tethered to the bed and rooted in place, pinned down and penetrated, Kingsley could have stayed there forever. But that was his arousal doing the talking. Or was it? Against the sheets, his cock throbbed. As Polly pushed into him, he pushed back. As she withdrew, he pushed down.

"Do you like it?" she whispered in his ear.

Do you like it?

Kingsley lowered his head with a groan and when he raised it again, he was far away in another time, another world. A shack—rough wood floors and walls. He was face-down, his wrists tied to the bars of a metal cot. A monster with blond hair and a brutal cock was on top of him, inside him. Earlier he'd been beaten with a black leather belt. By "accident" the blond monster had let go of the tip so that the sharp metal buckle hit him with the force of a whip and left a deep burning red welt on his ribcage that he already knew would turn into a black and blue bruise by the next day.

"Do you like it?" the monster asked as he fucked Kingsley for the second time that night. And because it was the second time, he was open and slick and there was no stopping the cock that pounded him.

"Yes, sir," Kingsley answered. Like it? His parents were dead. He was poor as a church mouse. His grandparents had sent him to an all-boys school against his will.

And as long as that cock kept ramming him, he couldn't have cared less. The cock made everything worth it.

God, he was such a whore.

"You're not allowed to like it this much," his monster decreed.

"Stop making it feel really fucking good then. Christ, do I have to explain everything?" Kingsley demanded. "You're supposed to be the smart one."

He only talked back like that when he was out of his mind from being fucked half to death.

Punishment came in the form of the blond monster's perfect pianist's fingers finding that throbbing welt on

Kingsley's back and pushing on it. Kingsley's head came up. He cried out in pain, in pain *and* in bliss. So much of both he couldn't tell one from the other.

"Stupid slut," his monster whispered into his ear. "You can't even suffer right."

"I love you, you fucking monster," Kingsley said. "I should be in my Calc study group right now."

Instead he had two dozen welts all over his back and a cock up his ass—which was exactly where it belonged, if you asked him.

"Shut the fuck up," the monster ordered. Victory…a dirty word. Kingsley had gotten to him. He would definitely not be shutting the fuck up now.

"I love you," Kingsley said again. "I fucking love you. I love your face and your body and your cock and that black hole in your chest where your heart's supposed to be. I want to die with you inside me I love you that fucking much."

"Really?" his monster said. "Every time I'm inside you, I want to kill you."

It was nine degrees outside the cabin, ninety degrees inside. Kingsley was drenched with sweat, open and wet as a whore on her last customer for the day, so hard he could have fucked a hole through the mattress. His legs and his beautiful monster's were tangled up together in the scattered sheets. One hand pushed on the welt. The other hand grasped Kingsley's long hair and pulled it.

Kingsley cried out as a muscle spasm rocketed up his spine.

"Why do I bother raping you?" the monster said and yanked Kingsley's hair again. "You enjoy it every time. What is even the point?"

"You want me to pretend to hate it? You want me to fight you off?" Kingsley asked. "I'll fight you."

Kingsley tried to fight him, tried to twist and push him

off. The result was…unsurprising. His monster did what monsters do. His monster bit him, bit the soft flesh between his neck and shoulder, the scruff, and Kingsley went limp like a kitten in its mother's teeth. But one good thing did happen from Kingsley's brief insurrection. He'd made his monster moan. Kingsley wasn't the only one enjoying this…

Kingsley laughed as he went limp on the cot again. His monster bit and licked the back of his neck as their bodies moved together. When Kingsley felt warm breath on his ear, the monster whispered, "Do you like it?"

"Kingsley?" Polly said again, her tone sharp enough to cut through the memory. "Do you like it?"

He grinned into the sheets. "Yes, ma'am."

Polly shifted herself upward and the phallus in him went deeper than it had gone before. Kingsley arched his back and let out a ragged groan as he took it. Polly held him by the shoulders as she fucked him. Now more rapidly, and rougher, too. It was what he wanted, what he needed and if she'd made him beg for it, he would have.

The pleasure grew so intense that at one point, he disassociated. His head swam, and he floated off the bed. He hung in the air, suspended by pure sensation. The harder she fucked him the higher he floated and when he crashed back to earth, he crashed hard. His back bowed, his fingers fisted the sheets, his thighs tightened to steel. He buried his face into the bedding and cried out as Polly pressed the phallus into him as far as it would go. Inside him muscles clenched and spasmed, clenched and released as he ground his cock into the bed and came in spurts onto the soft white sheets.

Done. Over. Kingsley went slack even as he lay sprawled, legs spread and still impaled on the bed.

"Tell me when," Polly said softly in his ear. "I'm not a man. I don't have to pull out immediately. I could stay in you all night."

"Don't leave. Not yet," he said. "Please."

"I'll wait until you tell me," she said and kissed his back again.

She stayed inside him as he basked for the span of a few breaths in the last little flutters of pleasure coursing through his body and blood. It was only when he felt pins and needles in his fingers did he nod the signal that he was ready for her to pull out of him.

Polly removed the ropes from his wrists. He murmured a grateful "*merci*" and she only kissed his cheek. He rolled onto his back, stretched like a well-fed house cat.

He heard her in the bathroom and then heard her in the bedroom again. His eyes were closed in spent exhaustion, but he wasn't quite ready to slip into sleep yet.

"My God," she said. "How much did you come?"

Kingsley opened his eyes. The wet spot on the bed was enormous.

"All of it," he said.

"I wish I'd weighed you before and after I fucked you," Polly said. "I bet you lost two kilos."

"I do feel lighter. At least my balls do."

"Don't worry. If they start floating, I'll tie them down."

Kingsley had no doubt she would.

She returned from the bathroom again with a clean white towel and draped it like a shroud over the massive come stain. "This," she said, "is why we make the men do the laundry."

"I thought it was because you enjoyed making men serve you."

"That, too," she said as she slid back into bed and pulled his arms around her. She was so soft and so warm, he could have fallen asleep against her immediately. "Isn't it funny? There are men in this world who would say you and I didn't have sex tonight because you never put your cock inside of

me. Wasn't what we just did so much more intense than standard-issue sex? The liter of semen would be Exhibit A."

He laughed softly, too tired to laugh loudly. He was as
spent as he'd been in a long time.

"Do you ever have standard-issue sex?" he asked.

"Oh, when the mood strikes me. I probably won't with
you. You're a little big for me. No offense."

"I'm deeply offended that you think my cock is too big.
Offend me some more, please."

———

THE STORY CONTINUES in The Chateau, *available now in
trade paperback, ebook, library hardcover, limited-edition signed-
and-numbered hardcover, and audio from 8th Circle Press and
Tantor Audio.*

GAUZE

THE COMPLETE SHORT STORY FROM "MICHAEL'S WINGS: COMPANION TO THE ANGEL"

This complete short story features Mistress Nora's favorite angel, Michael, and Griffin—his master, his true love, and the sexy-as-hell bane of his existence.

MICHAEL'S WINGS

Michael fucking hated gauze. But when he woke up it was the first thing he saw. Michael stared at the gauze on his wrists and tried not to remember, tried so hard not to remember. He didn't want to remember, didn't want to see the blood seeping through the gauze and turning the white cloth pink. It happened though, no matter how he tried to fight it. And before he could stop it, he found himself standing in the sanctuary of Sacred Heart again. And again he saw those crazy old bats at church who were pissed off at Father Stearns.

"I don't care how old and valuable the stained glass windows are," Father S had said. "I don't care if St. Peter himself donated them to Sacred Heart; if the glass breaks it's a safety hazard and the window will have to be replaced."

So much huffing and puffing from those old ladies followed. Someone's rich grandfather had donated the windows at Sacred Heart a hundred years ago. How dare Father Stearns suggest replacing the window? They whined so much that Father S had gathered them around and said, with a straight face that should have won him an Oscar, "If God wants the window to remain in the church, then God can heal the cracks in it Himself. If God wants it gone, he'll leave the job to the glazier. Start praying, ladies."

Usually Father S never got involved with such mundane issues at the church. He had a reputation for being a master delegator. But when it came to the safety of children, he always put his foot down. And when the foot of Father Stearns went down, it never came back up again.

Michael had told himself he was only going to look at the window out of curiosity. Father S had said during Sunday Mass that repairmen were coming to replace it that week. If he wanted to see the spectacularly cracked glass, he needed to do it now. His mom had been out in the entryway with Father S, talking to him in hushed and worried tones. Divorce…that's what they were talking about. His parents getting divorced. He didn't want to listen, didn't want to hear Father S telling his mom divorce was a sin and should be avoided at all costs. That's what their old priest said in the last town where they lived. If Father S said that to his mom, then maybe his mom would try to make up with his dad. That was the last thing he wanted. He'd rather live in a cardboard box than under the same roof as his dad again.

He'd rather die.

But what if his mom wanted to get back with his dad? She tried so hard, but they fought so much. Fought all the time. And always about him. Maybe he could run away and then they wouldn't fight anymore if he wasn't there. Maybe he could…

He'd stood in front of the stained-glass window and looked at the scene. He'd never really paid attention to this window before the big broken glass controversy. It depicted an angel standing proud and righteous with tall white wings that reached to the top of the sky, a flaming sword in its hands. A pretty scene. Too bad they'd have to get rid of it. A spiderweb of cracks had appeared at the bottom of the window, and one ran up the center all the way to the angel's chest; a six-foot crack had riven the glass. He ran a finger up one of the cracks, flinching as a sharp edge sliced his finger. A spot of blood appeared on the windowsill. For a few minutes, he could only stare at the spot as it darkened.

Again he touched the window and left a smear of red on the angel's foot. A piece of glass wiggled under his hand. He dug his fingers into the crack and a shard about four inches long broke off. When he looked down he saw more blood… not on the windowsill this time, but on the floor. Good thing it was hardwood. Should make it easier to clean.

When he looked up from the pooling blood, he saw

Father S rushing toward him, a look of pure terror on his face.

Father S? Terrified? That didn't make any sense. Nothing scared Father S.

"Michael…stay with me." He heard Father S's voice in the distance, even though he knew his priest only stood a few feet away. "Help is coming. Don't fall asleep. Stay awake. Talk to me."

"I'll clean the floor," Michael said, but wasn't sure if he said it out loud. He looked up and saw Father S holding him by both wrists. Where had all the blood on Father S's hands come from? Had he cut himself on the window, too?

A mile away he heard a woman screaming. He closed his eyes. When he woke up, he saw gauze.

"Mick? Come on, Mick? Come back to me."

He blinked a few times and looked away from the gauze and into Griffin's hazel eyes. Griffin snapped his fingers again and Michael sat up, pulling the sheets up to his hips. He wasn't quite used to being totally naked in front of someone other than Nora yet.

"I'm sorry, sir." The "sir" came easier than the being naked part did. Michael laughed a little and rubbed his forehead.

"Don't be sorry." Griffin put his hand on the side of Michael's neck. "You want to tell me where you were? Your eyes were open and I said your name about twenty times. You scared the shit out of me."

"I'm sorry. Really sorry. I just woke up and saw the gauze…" He held up his wrists, freshly tattooed and gauze-covered. "It brought back memories."

"Bad ones?" Griffin furrowed his brow. Michael didn't like that look. Griffin was gorgeous no matter what look he had on his face, but when he smiled, it was like a bomb went off in the room. A happiness bomb. Nervous, worried—those weren't good looks for him.

"Pretty bad. I'm sorry," Michael said again. "This is our first night in your bed together and I'm being all emo again."

"I love my emo-Mick." Griffin bent forward and kissed him. "You can be as emo as you need to be when you need to be. But if I see you disappearing on me again, I'm going to drag you back to me by your hair if I have to. Fair?" Griffin tugged on his hair hard enough to make the point. The fog of the bad memories had already started to dissipate in Griffin's presence.

"Fair." After all, he could hardly linger in the past when the present moment involved him and a naked Griffin in the biggest, softest, most luxurious bed he'd ever slept in. "I'll try not to go back there. Promise."

"Is gauze a trigger?"

Michael shrugged. Griffin rolled his eyes and sighed before smiling again. He reached out and dragged Michael to him and slammed them both down into the bed.

"Repeat after me, sub," Griffin said, dragging Michael back against his chest. "Ready?"

"*Ready.*"

"Smartass."

"*Smartass.*"

Michael cried out in pain as Griffin bit him hard on the back of the shoulder. The pain sent adrenaline shooting through his body and immediately he felt better. He was even a little turned on.

"I deserved that," Michael said as he relaxed into Griffin's arms.

"You did. Repeat after me: 'I am not a clam.' "

"What?"

"Just say it."

Michael exhaled heavily. "*I am not a clam.*"

"I am a person."

"*I am a person.*"

"I answer the questions that my owner, the devastatingly handsome and charming Griffin Randolfe Fiske, asks me to answer…"

"I answer the questions that my owner, the devastatingly handsome and charming Griffin Randolfe Fiske, asks me to answer..." Michael managed to say all of that without laughing, which made him pretty proud of himself.

"Because I am a person and not a clam."

"Because I am a person and not a clam."

"So stop clamming up." Griffin punctuated the order with another bite. This time the pain also sent blood surging through his body. He felt Griffin starting to get hard against his hip. "I own you, remember? This isn't a game. I can't take care of you if you don't tell me what's going on in your head."

Griffin knocked on Michael's skull like it was a door needing opened. Michael laughed and groaned simultaneously.

"Yes, okay. Gauze is kind of a trigger. I'm alright, I promise."

He'd spent all summer working with Nora on some of his fears and bad memories, on coping techniques to deal with his triggers. Nora had even gotten him to the point he could hold razor blades and other sharp objects without feeling freaked out. Before this summer with Nora, even scissors and butter knives had made his hands a little shaky. He'd forgotten to tell her about the gauze.

"No sub of mine is going to let a Band-Aid beat him. Only I get to beat you. Right?"

"Yes, sir."

"Which is why you're going to talk to me about stuff like this all the time. Because we're together now. I own you. So that means I own your stuff. The bad stuff and the good stuff. It's all mine, just like you're all mine. Got it?"

"I got it."

"So give it up."

Michael took a deep breath. He opened his mouth and then closed it again.

"Mick…" Griffin nipped at the back of Michael's neck and placed a kiss on top of the bite. "I'm not going to fuck you again or let you come until you tell me what's going on."

"Okay, so the gauze," Michael began, the words rushing out at breakneck pace, "I slit my wrists, both of them. I don't even remember doing it. I only remember the blood and my mom screaming and Father S trying to keep me conscious. I remember waking up and seeing gauze on my wrists. I lived in gauze for months after that. I couldn't even look when my mom changed the bandages. I closed my eyes and turned my head. I didn't see the scars until three months after I got out of the hospital. All I saw was the gauze."

Michael remembered burying his head against his mom's shoulder as she washed his stitches and changed his bandages night after night. She never said anything during those humiliating tortures at the bathroom sink. She'd work in silence, sometimes crying, sometimes not. Only at the end when it was over would she kiss him on the cheek and tell him she loved him. Once his wrists had healed, she didn't have to deal with the wound washing anymore. Michael almost missed it by then. It was the one time of day he felt close to his mom.

"So gauze makes you think bad things?" Griffin asked, running his hand over Michael's arm from shoulder to wrist and back up again.

"It makes me remember. That's all. I'll get over it. Just… bad associations."

"Bad associations. I get it. I do. I got alcohol poisoning once on absinthe and—"

"Absinthe? I thought that was illegal?"

"It is. So is coke too, but that didn't stop me from getting fistfuls of it and shoving it up my nose. Anyway, absinthe had this sort of licorice flavor to it. I can't even smell licorice now without wanting to puke my guts out. That's good though. That bad association will keep me from ever drinking it or any other alcohol again. But you just got some serious ink on your wrists so you'll need the gauze for a few days."

"I know. I know… I'll be okay." Michael took a quick and determined breath. "I'll deal with it."

"No, *we'll* deal with it."

Griffin pushed Michael onto his back. Michael wound his arms around Griffin's shoulders as they kissed long and deep, their tongues mingling, their hips pressing into each other. Fucking was a much better idea than talking about Michael's bad associations with gauze.

A low rumbling noise emanated from the area of their stomachs and both he and Griffin paused mid-kiss.

"Wait…" Griffin pulled up and looked down at Michael. "Was that your stomach growling or mine?"

"I don't know. I couldn't tell."

"Are you hungry?"

"Starving. But I can wait." Michael hadn't eaten since last night, before the big drama explosion with Griffin running off to confront Father S.

Was that just last night? It seemed like another lifetime, like his entire existence needed to be divided into two parts: Before-Sex-With-Griffin and After-Sex-With-Griffin. This morning he'd woken up in Griffin's bed and they'd had sex for the first time. Then the second time. They'd fallen asleep again and when he'd woken up, he'd seen the gauze staring him down.

"You can wait, but I can't," Griffin said. "I turn into a bear when hungry. Wait. Not a bear. Bad choice of words. I don't suddenly look like a huge gay man with tons of body hair, do I?"

Michael pretended to study him. No excess body hair at all and not an ounce of fat on all those muscles. "No, you're good. You still look metrosexual."

"Thank God. I'm a busy trust fund baby without a real job. I don't have time to get my back waxed. Come on, let's get some food. I'll fuck you later."

"But not much later, right?"

"I mean like in half an hour. Can you wait that long?"

Michael mulled it over. "I'll try. No promises," he said with a ragged, melodramatic sigh.

Griffin laughed as he leaned across Michael and hit the call button on his intercom.

"Alfred!" Griffin yelled loudly enough the intercom box momentarily screamed with feedback. "Are you still awake?"

"No," came the response. Jamison, Griffin's butler, sounded irritated and murderous as usual. "I've died and you are here, Master Griffin. I am in hell."

"Good," Griffin said, not sounding remotely insulted by his butler's bad attitude. "Could you run into Hell's Kitchen and make us some grilled cheeses? Like with the fancy cheese? And some fruit and healthy shit?"

"Yes, Master Griffin. I will use the 'fancy' cheese. And rat poison."

"Extra cheese on mine," Griffin said. "Mick? That sound okay?"

"Sounds great." He was hungry enough he'd even eat non-fancy cheese with rat poison.

"Mick's fine with that."

"I'm pleased to hear your infant approves of the midnight snack selection."

"Can we have orange juice, too?" Griffin asked, winking at Michael. The thought of sixty-something Jamison knowing that he and Griffin were in bed together was slightly mortifying.

"No, you may not. Orange juice is liquid candy," Jamison replied.

"It's good for rehydration. I looked it up on Wiki."

"Wikipedia," Jamison began, his voice dripping with disgust, "is not a resource for researching one's moral quandaries. It is pornography for pseudo-intellectuals."

"Make that two OJ's," Griffin said.

"I pray nightly for the end of your tyranny, Master Griffin."

"Thanks, we'll be down in the dining room in fifteen."

Griffin hit the call button again and the intercom went silent. Griffin threw the sheets off and started gathering their discarded clothes.

"Why does your butler hate you so much?" Michael asked as Griffin tossed him his boxers and t-shirt.

"Alfred? He doesn't hate me."

"He acts like it."

"It only sounds like he hates me because he's British."

Griffin pulled his jeans on and buttoned them, not bothering with underwear. Michael experienced a brief and wonderful fugue state as he stared at Griffin's flat and muscular stomach and that little line of hair disappearing into his low-slung jeans. He even had a little hipbone sticking out. Food… What food?

"Mick?" Griffin snapped his fingers.

"I'm here, I swear. I wasn't in a bad place." Michael forced himself to meet Griffin's eyes.

"Where were you?" Griffin sounded suspicious.

"In your pants."

"Oh…that's okay then. Dinner?"

"Dinner."

Jamison had their food waiting for them on the table in the dining room. He'd apparently cooked and returned to bed, so they were not greeted by his ever-charming presence.

"Oh my fucking God…" Griffin groaned as he finished his sandwich. "I love fancy cheese."

"It's amazing." Michael ate a little more slowly than Griffin. He sipped at his orange juice as he watched Griffin peel grapes off a stem and pop them into his mouth. "Are you sure it's not poisoned?"

"Nope."

"I'm still going to eat this sandwich though."

"I would. I did. I'm going to see if there's any more left."

Michael sat back and pulled his feet into the chair as he peeled the crusts off the grilled cheese. Alone at the table, Michael finished eating. He felt entirely calm now, at peace, contented. He still couldn't believe this had all happened… that Griffin had fallen in love with him and they'd slept together and Griffin even seemed determined they were going to be together now and no one could or would stop them. Nora had even left them earlier that day, left them alone, left Michael in Griffin's care. She saw them as a couple. It was real.

"Are you done eating?" Griffin asked from behind Michael's chair.

"Yeah. That was awesome. Even if Jamison did poison the food, it was a great last meal."

"Want some dessert?"

Michael looked up and saw Griffin standing behind the chair with a wicked smile on his face.

"You're not talking about food, are you?"

Griffin shook his head slowly. The smile got wickeder.

"You know I call this the anal table, right?"

"Right…"

"You want to find out why I call it the anal table?"

Griffin took a few steps back, shut the dining room door and locked it behind him. He seemed to have something in his hands.

"Clear the table, Mick," Griffin ordered and Michael rose immediately and started gathering all the plates. He stacked them on the sideboard as Griffin stood by the table and waited, watching him. He'd have to get used to this, jumping at Griffin's command to do whatever he was told. He could get used to this. Truth be told he probably already was used to it.

"Good boy," Griffin said once the table was clear and clean. Griffin crooked his finger at Michael and pointed at the table.

Okay, yeah, he was definitely used to this.

He went to the end of the table and waited. Griffin stood in front of him and put something down behind Michael's back. Michael started to look but Griffin raised his chin.

"Your eyes on my eyes," Griffin said and Michael obeyed.

"Yes, sir."

Michael already felt his blood starting to stir.

"Listen to me…" Griffin gathered Michael's t-shirt in his hands and lifted, pulling it off and tossing it on the floor. He ran his hands up and down Michael's shoulders, chest, and stomach. "I'm going to tie you up and I'm going to fuck you. And I'm going to use this to tie you up, okay?" He reached behind Michael and held up a roll of white gauze.

"You are?" Michael's stomach tightened.

"I am. You can safe out now and we'll just go back upstairs and fuck in my bed. But if we're going to do it here we'll use the gauze. You need some better associations. I want to give you and gauze one good, long, hard ass…..ociation. How does that sound?"

"Amazing, sir."

"Good. Get naked."

Michael slid his boxer shorts off and kicked them aside. Griffin pushed him back onto the table. The cool polished wood beneath his back made him acutely aware of his own body.

Griffin went to the sideboard and opened a drawer. He brought a bottle of lube over and set it next to Michael's hip.

"You keep lube in the dining room?" Michael asked, as Griffin started to unwind a few feet of gauze.

"Trust me, the anal table has earned its name." Griffin grabbed Michael by the forearm and wound two feet of gauze around his already-wrapped wrists. "Tell me if anything gets too tight," Griffin said as he wrapped the gauze around one table leg.

"It's good. I promise, I—" Michael said, but Griffin had disappeared. "Wait. Where—?"

"I'm here." Griffin popped up on the other side of the table. He'd gone under it with the gauze to get to the other side. He took Michael's other wrist and wound the gauze around it.

"Pull a little," Griffin said. Michael tugged, feeling the give in the gauze but also the strength of it. He couldn't get out without cutting it. That was fine. He was okay. Not scared. Not scared at all. "Plenty of give?"

"Yes, sir."

"Good. Now stay there." Griffin gave him a wink that caused Michael to melt like candlewax onto the table. "It's good for the gauze to have some stretch to it since I need to move you…right…here."

With a gentle tug, Griffin pulled Michael by his thighs to the very edge of the table.

"Pull your knees to your chest," Griffin ordered and Michael obeyed, feeling embarrassed and self-conscious as Griffin applied the lube to him. It felt so weird just lying there while Griffin prepped him. This act, more than anything else so far, made him feel like a piece of property, a body to be used by Griffin for his pleasure, not Michael's.

And for some reason that made no sense in his mind but perfect sense to his heart and his body. Being used for Griffin's pleasure gave Michael more pleasure, not less. The more he gave up of himself, the more he got in return.

He started to relax as Griffin inserted two fingers and then three, gently thrusting them in and out. Griffin knew all the right ways to touch him inside.

"You're really good at that," Michael said between breaths.

"I've had some practice."

"Have you…" Michael couldn't bring himself to ask the rest of the question.

"Bottomed?" Griffin could apparently speak the language of embarrassed. "Yeah, when I was younger. Never really loved it though. Born to give."

"Born to take." Michael smiled at him.

"You're totally thinking about it now, aren't you? Me getting it up the ass?"

"I really am," Michael said as Griffin opened his jeans and freed his erection. He'd seen a couple pictures of Griffin in his teens and early twenties. Just as gorgeous but with a lot less muscle. "Anyone I know?"

"Let's just say the very last time was about seven years ago. I sort of failed Kingsley's 'Have you ever had sex in the back of a Rolls Royce?' test."

"Awesome."

Michael started to laugh but the laugh died as Griffin started to push into him. For whatever reason–the force, the thrust, the type of lube–the sex felt mind-blowingly good, better than it had even the first and second times they'd done this today.

"God…" Michael's back arched off the table.

"Told you this was the anal table for a reason. It's got ass magic, I have no idea why."

"I think it's the angle. Good thrusting angle."

"Good *fucking* angle," Griffin corrected and Michael smiled at the ceiling.

He closed his eyes as Griffin started to move in him harder and deeper. Every thrust worked that magic on him. With each stroke Griffin ran his hands up and down Michael's thighs.

Griffin gave a shuddering breath as he dug his fingers into Michael's skin. "You feel so good, this should be illegal."

"What if it was?"

"I don't care. I'd go to the chair for this."

"The chair…like for chair sex?" Michael suggested, raising his head off the table to smile at him.

"Chair sex is on our to do list."

Griffin thrust a few more times before pulling completely out of Michael.

"Come here, sub. I want a new fucking angle."

Michael laughed as Griffin dragged him off the table. The gauze stretched just far enough for Michael to stand at the end of the table with his hips against the edge and his chest and stomach flat on the wood. As soon as Griffin had him in place, he pushed into him again.

"God damn…" Griffin groaned as he clamped a hand onto the back of Michael's neck and proceeded to shake the table with thrusts.

Michael could do nothing but relax and take everything Griffin had to give him. Through the haze of sex and sweat, Michael stared at the gauze wrapped around his wrists. It was pretty really, the white crisscrossing pattern, the fabric the color of snow. It was soft, too. Every time he saw it from now on he'd think of this moment bent over a table with the sexiest, funniest, most incredible guy on earth inside him making him feel amazing ten times over.

Griffin's breathing grew heavier, more desperate. His hands scored Michael's back. The pain brought Michael nearly to orgasm, but he held back knowing he shouldn't come without Griffin's permission.

The final few thrusts were so hard they almost hurt. Michael closed his eyes tight as he took them. With a soft grunt, Griffin came inside him. He pulled out slowly and Michael did nothing but lay there on the table breathing.

"Okay," Griffin said, caressing Michael's side from his hip to his shoulder. "That was pretty incredible. Was that incredible for you, too? Because I think my cock is ringing. Is that normal? I don't care. Never mind. Rhetorical question."

Griffin brought out a sharp kitchen knife from the sideboard and sliced through the gauze. He did it far away from Michael, a consideration Michael greatly appreciated. As soon as Michael was free he stood up on shaking legs. Griffin stood behind him and wrapped him up in his tattooed arms.

Griffin started to stroke Michael's erection. "I think we forgot something…"

"I hadn't forgotten," Michael said, turning his head for a kiss. "My dick won't let me forget something like that."

"We better head to the living room to take care of this then."

Griffin turned Michael to face him and they lost themselves in one more kiss.

"What's in the living room?" Michael asked as Griffin bit and kissed his neck.

"The oral ottoman."

———

READ MORE Michael and Griffin in Michael's Wings, *available now in trade paperback, ebook, library hardcover, and audio from 8th Circle Press and Tantor Audio.*

YOUNG WINE

EXCERPT FROM "THE SAINT," THE FIFTH
BOOK IN THE ORIGINAL SINNERS SERIES

Mistress Nora tracks down Kingsley's long-lost son. Nicolas "Nico" Delacroix turns out to be young, strikingly handsome, and very French. He wants nothing to do with his father...but everything to do with Nora.

TIFFANY REISZ

The
SAINT

The shut the door behind Nico and pulled him to the fireplace. She helped him out of his jacket and boots. Battered and mud-crusted, his shoes looked nothing like Kingsley's spit-shined riding boots. These were work boots, steel-tipped and utilitarian.

"Do I want to know how you found me?" she asked as she brushed the mud off Nico's boots and set them to dry by the fireplace.

"I followed your trail of bread crumbs."

"Bread crumbs?"

"You might have accidentally left your bag open at the restaurant and I might have accidentally seen the address on your rental confirmation."

"Leaving my bag open *was* an accident," she said.

"Finding the address might not have been." He pulled off his socks and ran his hands through his hair, shaking the rain out of it.

"Like father, like son," she sighed. "You're as sneaky as Kingsley."

"Are you angry?"

"No, I'm not angry." She raised her hand to her forehead and rubbed at the tension headache lurking there. Nico pulled her hand down and looked at her with concern.

"Need food? Wine?" she asked before he could ask her how she was—a question she didn't want to answer. "Or did you bring your own?"

"There might be a bottle or two of Rosanella in the car."

"I won't make you bring them in," she said. Outside the storm still raged wild.

"I will later. First things first." Nico took her by the wrist and pulled her close.

"Nico…"

"Don't," he said. "Don't fight me. Let me help you."

Sighing, Nora rested her head against his chest and let

him rub the knot of tension in her neck. When they met in December she'd had Zach with her, and Nico—only his mother called him Nicholas, he'd said—had shown her editor/friend/occasional lover all due deference. But when she visited again a month later, Nico did nothing to hide his delight at having her to himself. He was barely twenty-five. Handsome and young and French, what reason did he have for wanting her—nearly twelve years his senior and with a long history of sleeping with the man he'd learned was his biological father? She got her answer while they were out walking one day. Two women—a mother and daughter—had stopped them, asking for directions. The mother looked forty years old, the daughter around Nico's age. Both were well-dressed classic French beauties. Nico barely blinked at the daughter. To the mother he'd flashed a smile so flirtatious even his father would have been impressed. Kingsley's son had a fetish for older women.

Well…how nice.

"You're in pain," he said. "I can feel it all through you."

"I like pain," she reminded him.

"No one likes this kind of pain. I would know."

She lowered her eyes in sympathy. The man who raised Nico as his son had died five months ago. A month after that, she'd shown up and told him he had another father, which had torn the stitches on his still-healing grief. If anyone understood the pain she felt right now, it was Nico.

"Let me ease your pain tonight."

"How?" She looked up at him. "Can you bring people back to life?"

"I can bring *you* back to life."

She almost told him he was as arrogant as his father, but before she could speak, he kissed her.

Nervous as a virgin, her lips trembled under his. If it had been anyone but him, she would have wondered at this newfound shyness. She'd never been shy, never been demure, never been innocent. And yet, this was Kingsley's only son, and by sleeping with him she would lose something far more dear to her then her virginity had ever been.

"You're shaking," Nico said against her lips.

"I'm scared."

"Scared? Why?"

"I don't know."

"I'm here," he whispered. "You don't have to be afraid."

He was here. That's why she was afraid. But the fear didn't stop her from opening her mouth to receive his kiss. He kissed along her jawline to her ear, nipped at her earlobe. Over the pulse point in her neck he pressed a long languid kiss. The heat from his mouth seared her all the way to her spine. His kisses were neither tentative nor hurried. As he kissed her, her muscles slackened, her skin flushed with heat, and the fear faded. For the first time in days, she felt human. Since meeting back in December, she and Nico had been in weekly contact. Emails, phone calls—he even wrote her letters by hand. Letters she read and reread and answered. Letters she burned before anyone found them.

Her head fell back as Nico kissed the hollow of her throat. He placed his hands on either side of her neck and rubbed his thumbs into the tendons of her shoulders.

"What's this?" he asked as he lifted the chain of her necklace.

Nora wrapped her hand around the pendant. She couldn't talk about it yet. It meant too much to her. Especially now.

"A saint medal. It's a Catholic thing."

"I know about saints. I am one, remember?".

"Saint Nicholas brought me Christmas early this year," she said, smiling as he kissed her throat. "Although sleeping with him will put me on the naughty list for eternity."

"It's my list. I'll be the judge of that." He slipped the strap of her nightgown off her shoulder and traced her bare shoulder with his fingertips. Her body shivered with the pleasure from the touch of his work-roughened skin.

"You're so beautiful in white." Nico whispered the words into her ear as he ran his hand down her back caressing the silk of her gown.

Nora said nothing. She'd bought the white gown to wear for Søren on their anniversary, a celebration that wouldn't happen now.

She released the medal and it fell once more against her skin. She wrapped her arms around Nico's broad shoulders and pressed her breasts to his chest. He wore a basic black cotton T-shirt and work jeans. She wore a silk nightgown. He'd been working all day and had come to her with mud on his boots. She'd been mourning all week and came to him with sorrow in her heart.

"I want to spend all night inside you," Nico breathed against her neck.

She pulled away from his embrace but only to take him by the hand.

"Come upstairs," she said. "We can sleep when we're dead."

She led him up to the bedroom. He released her hand to tend to the fading fire. He fed it with paper first, then kindling, then threw a log on top of the smoldering flames. The room warmed and glowed red from the heat and firelight.

"You're good at that," Nora said. "Do you have a fireplace at your house?"

"Two of them," he said. *Two of zem.* Nora bit the inside of her mouth to keep from laughing. She'd learned from Nico that he'd spent a year in California and another year in Australia in his teens. Even though he lived in France now, he'd mastered

English to the point that his accent was faint. Still there, but certainly not as pronounced as Kingsley's deliberately exaggerated accent. But every now and then Nico's accent came out in full force. "You should come to my home. I'd like you to see it."

She'd refused all invitations to come to his home and instead met him in neutral locations—Arles, Marseille. She knew once they were alone together in his house or hers this would happen. And so it had.

"If I come to your house, will you put me to work?" she asked as she came to stand next to him. The fire crackled and a burning ash landed near her foot. Nico brushed it away with his bare hand.

"Everyone works at Rosanella."

"I still can't believe you are what you are."

"Why not?" He smiled up at her.

"Kingsley does not get his hands dirty. Not in the literal sense anyway."

"You think he's ashamed that I'm a farmer?"

"You make wine. He drinks wine. He's proud of you."

Whether he'd admit it or not, Kingsley had fallen in love with the idea of being Nico's father. "My son the vintner," he said sometimes, and Nora saw the pride in his eyes. It broke her heart that Nico had yet to feel any pride that Kingsley was his father.

"And you?" Nico looked up at her from where he knelt on the floor. "Are you proud of me?"

"Does it matter?"

"It matters more that you're proud of me than him."

She caressed his face with the back of her hand. The slight stubble on his chin chafed her skin. Once she'd asked him what he was looking for every time he went to bed with a woman ten, fifteen, twenty years older than he. A mother figure? A teacher? A trainer? "My Rosanella," Nico had answered, referring to the name of his vineyard's bestselling Syrah, "the one woman who is all women."

"Yes, my Nico. I'm proud of you."

They gazed at each other. The shutters were closed. Fire alone warmed and brightened the room. Outside the wind and rain poured and howled so wildly she imagined everyone but she and Nico had been wiped off the face of the earth. Only they two remained, sole survivors.

Nico rose up on his knees, put his hands on her waist and kissed her stomach through the fabric of her gown. Slowly he slid his hands down the backs of her legs and grasped her ankles. Nora buried her fingers in his hair as he kissed her bare thigh where it peeked out of the hip-high slit in her nightgown. He ran his hands back up her legs. Everything he did, every way he touched her, set her nerves tingling and her stomach tightening. Now with his thumbs he parted the slit of her gown. Nora grasped the bedpost behind her as Nico pressed a kiss onto the apex of her thighs. She pushed her hips forward as Nico sought her clitoris with his tongue.

"What's this?" he asked, tickling the little metal hoop he'd found.

"Clit ring."

Nico raised an eyebrow.

"I'm going to play with that later."

"You can play with it now."

She opened her legs wider, and he slid one finger between her wet seam and inside her. He hooked his finger over her pubic bone and ground his fingertip into the soft indention he found there.

He teased her with his tongue before sucking on her clitoris in earnest. She leaned against the footboard behind her to steady herself. The room carried the heady scent of smoke. The heat from the fire stoked her own inner heat. She could hear Nico's ragged breaths as he licked and kissed her.

He turned his hand and pushed a second finger inside her. He spread his fingers apart, opening her up for him. Her inner muscles twitched around his hand. It was too much. She couldn't wait anymore.

"Stop," she ordered. Nico obeyed and rested back on his hands. She grasped the fabric of his T-shirt and he raised his arms. He unbuttoned his jeans as she tossed his shirt to the floor. Hard muscles lurked under his clothes—muscles he'd earned working the vineyard and not at a gym. He put those muscles to use as he rose up and pulled her hard against him. She felt his erection pressing against her. She raised one leg and wrapped it around his back, opening herself up to him. The tip went in easily and Nico lifted her and brought her down onto him, impaling her. It was only a few steps to the bed and he carried her there, laying her on her back across the burgundy coverlet.

Nico covered her body with his and drove into her with a slow sensuous thrust that sent ecstasy radiating from her back to her fingers. He pulled out to the tip and pushed back in again, her wet body giving him no resistance. He showed total mastery of his desire as he moved in her, advancing, retreating, performing the ancient steps of this primal dance with powerful male grace. He seemed in no hurry to come, as if he fully intended to stay inside her all night. She ran her hands down the length of his torso and let them rest at the small of his back. She could feel his taut muscles working as his back bowed every time he entered her and arched with each retreat.

With every thrust, Nora raised her hips to meet his. The base of his penis grazed her clitoris, and she lifted her head to kiss and bite his shoulders. Fluid ran out of her, glazing her inner thighs. She lifted her knees to open herself even more to him. She breathed in and inhaled his scent—warm and alive, like the new spring that surrounded them in the forest.

He slipped his hand between their bodies. She shivered beneath him, her head falling back against the bed as he grasped her swollen clitoris between his fingertips and stroked it. He pushed forcefully into her, and Nora gasped as her inner muscles clenched around him.

The world went still and silent around them. Nora couldn't even hear the storm anymore, the crackling of the fireplace, the creaking of the bed. All she could hear was the quiet metallic jangling of Nico's belt, his ragged breaths and the sound of her wetness.

Every part of her body went tight as Nico bore down on her and came inside her with a shudder. He pulled out and kissed a path down her chest and stomach. With his head between her thighs he lapped at her clitoris again. Her back tensed, her stomach quivered, and she inhaled and forgot to breathe out. He pushed his fingers into her dripping body and sent her over the edge. Every muscle inside her spasmed violently. She hadn't had sex in so long that it felt as though a week's worth of orgasms thundered through her all at once.

Nico's semen spilled out of her and onto the bed. Nora wrapped her arms around him as he relaxed on top of her, covering her neck and shoulders in carnal kisses.

"Thank you," she said. "I needed that."

"So did I. I've needed it for months."

He kissed her long and deep on the mouth before pulling himself up.

He crawled off the bed and grabbed his shirt off the floor. She watched him pull himself back together. She'd always loved this part, watching a man dress after sex. She loved the perfunctory way Nico pulled on his shirt as if it never occurred to him she would be watching him and enjoying the view.

"Where are you going?"

"You need to drink my wine. Want some?"

"Nico, if you came in a cup I would drink it."

He stared at her. Had she actually made the son of Kingsley Edge blush?

"We'll save that vintage for later."

———

THE STORY CONTINUES in The Saint, *available now in trade paperback, ebook, and audio from Harlequin's Mira Books and Mills & Boon.*

TURNDOWN SERVICE

EXCERPT FROM "PICTURE PERFECT COWBOY," A STANDALONE EROTIC WESTERN ROMANCE

Jason "Still" Waters' life looks perfect from the outside—money, fame, and the words "World Champion Bull-Rider" after his name. But Jason has a secret, one he never planned on telling anybody...until he meets Simone. She's the kinky girl of his dreams...and his conservative family's worst nightmare.

PICTURE PERFECT
Cowboy

J ason put his hands around Simone's waist and stood her in front of him. Some sort of trance had come over him. His hands weren't even shaking as he unbuttoned Simone's jeans and pushed them slowly down her legs.

He wasn't too surprised to find she wore pink lacy thong panties under her ripped and faded jeans. They were so frilly and feminine and looked so pretty on her full hips that he dipped his head and kissed the little bow at the center. She liked that. He could tell from the way she breathed in when his lips met her skin. If she were his all the time, day and night, he'd make sure she always wore little frilly things under her regular clothes, for his eyes only. He stayed close to her body as he slid her jeans all the way down her calves. He tapped her ankles to signal for her to step out of them. Her panties were so pretty he didn't want to take them off of her yet. Instead he stood up and turned her toward the kitchen table.

"Bend over," he said. She did immediately, obeying the order like she'd been waiting for it.

Jason knew he'd never seen anything in the world to rival the sight of a girl wearing his flannel shirt and pink thong panties bent over his kitchen table. Standing behind her, he put his hand flat on the nicest ass he'd seen in his twenty-nine years and pinched it. He didn't pinch hard, not at first. He still couldn't quite believe he was doing all this without her saying a word to stop him. He pinched her harder, hard enough to leave a red mark behind on her pale skin. She flinched but didn't say a word.

"Spread your legs wide," he said.

Gracefully, she lifted her right foot and, with her toe pointed like a ballerina, placed it onto the floor, leaving a good foot and a half between her ankles. Without waiting for his order, she arched her back, which lifted her hips. An invitation. He accepted it. He hooked his finger under the edge of her thong and slid it down, down, over the curve of her soft ass and down to her pussy, which was bare of hair and warm against his knuckles. He pushed the crotch of her panties over to the side. She was pink here, too, pink and red and wet enough he could see it shimmer. He spread her wider with his fingers, spread her wide enough he was worried he might be hurting her. She groaned a little, but it didn't seem to be a groan of pain.

"Pretty pussy. Pretty ass," he said and couldn't believe those words came out of the same mouth that sang hymns every Sunday morning at the First Presbyterian Church.

Simone said nothing and he wondered if he'd gone too far.

"You don't say thank you when a man pays you a compliment like that?" he asked.

"I'll say anything you tell me to, sir," she said. Her voice was small and girlish, almost timid and sweet as pie.

Sir.

Jason closed his eyes and let that word wash all over him like healing water. "Sir?" he repeated.

"Would you prefer I call you Master Jason?" she asked.

Would he? He might, but he might also faint if she did. He was so hard already that if she got him any harder he'd pass out from loss of blood in the brain.

"Sir is just fine," he said. "Now I want you to say thank you when I pay you a compliment."

"Thank you, sir," she said. He could tell she meant it.

"Good girl."

He wanted to go inside her and he wanted to do it without asking permission first. He wanted to stick his fingers in her like he had every right to do it, like he was a man walking into a house he'd paid for in cash. She had said he could, and there was only one way to find out if she meant it. Jason pushed three fingers into her vagina. He went in slow but not too slow. He pressed firmly, purpose-fully, and all the way up to the knuckles. Simone's pussy clenched around his fingers but not to push him out. She didn't say her safe word. Instead she moaned a long, low "fuck…"

"I don't like language like that from my girl," he said. "That's not how ladies talk."

"I'm sorry, sir," she said, breathless.

"I'm gonna have to punish you for that. Just so you'll remember for next time."

"Yes, sir," she said.

Jason pulled his fingers out of her and the way she groaned, he wondered if that was punishment enough. Maybe for her, but not for him. He stood to the side of her hip and lifted his hand, ready to swat her ass. He stopped, hand a foot from her flesh. This was it. First time in his life he ever raised his hand to strike a woman. A wave of dizzi-ness hit him. He felt momentarily sick to his stomach. Then Simone spoke again, in her sweet, tender voice.

"I deserve it," she said. "And I want to learn to be better."

She must have sensed his hesitation, sensed the reason for it.

"There's two ways to do things," he said. "My way and your way. We're going to do things my way. You understand?"

"Yes, sir."

He raised his hand higher, two feet from her flesh. She arched her back again, lifting her hips once more. Another invitation. Once more, he accepted it. He slapped her hard, a sharp slap, right on the center of her left cheek. It made a loud quick sound, almost like a pop, and when he looked down at her, he saw the red outline of his hand on her skin. It looked so sexy on her, that handprint, that he gave her one on the right cheek, as well.

After, Jason had to stop and take a few deep breaths to calm himself down.

"Now that wasn't so bad, was it?" he asked, asking himself and her at the same time.

"No, sir."

Jason allowed himself a few more breaths to settle down. He felt drunk, stoned, manic and high and all at the same time. He needed to get control of himself and fast. He had a girl to take care of and he couldn't take care of her if he wasn't in complete control of himself.

"Stand up," he said. Simone stood. He took her by the waist and turned her to face him. They were hip to hip and chest to chest but not eye to eye. She kept her eyes lowered, out of respect.

"You're gonna do a couple things for me right now," he said. She nodded, agreeing before he'd even told her what to do. "You're gonna go out that door over there and through the living room. You'll go up the stairs. At the top of the stairs there's a bathroom and two bedrooms. I want you in the blue bedroom. When you get up there, you're going to turn the bed down, nice and neat. Understand?"

"Nice and neat," she repeated. "Yes, sir."

"There's a rug on the floor. I want you to kneel on it with your back to the door and wait for me. It'll be a few minutes, but I'll be there real soon. Go on now." He snapped his fingers and pointed.

Without another word she padded from the kitchen in her white socks and out the door he'd shown her. He heard her on the steps, going quick, which made him grin. When he gave an order, she hopped to it.

Jason sat down at the kitchen table and stared at the floor where Simone's jeans laid in a pile at his feet. Proof. Proof this was really happening. He put his elbows on the table and rested his face in the cradle of his hands. He inhaled the scent of Simone's body on his fingers. He'd done it. He'd hit a girl with his own hands and the world hadn't ended. He looked for his guilt, his shame, couldn't find it anywhere. That was nice. It had run off and hid for the day. He knew he'd see it again before long but for now, he'd enjoy his time without it.

After one more deep breath, Jason stood up. He felt calm but excited, like he always felt before a ride. He might have ridden eighteen-hundred-pound bulls but nothing had scared him quite like taking those steps upstairs to the guest room where he'd sent Simone. He looked through the door and saw she'd done everything he'd ordered. The bed was neatly turned back, she knelt on the floor, and she wore just her underwear and his shirt, which she'd knotted under her breasts. He left her on the floor waiting while he went into his bedroom and found the box of condoms under his bathroom sink. That wasn't all he wanted, though. In his closet, way in the back corner, he found a riding crop he'd bought at a horse tack store in California, one of the fancy ones that sold dressage and show-jumping equipment. He'd been drawn to the crop at first sight. A jumping bat, it was called. Shorter than a regular riding crop with a wide flapper at the end, big as his palm and smooth brown leather. The lady had asked him if he trained show horses, and he'd lied and said he did.

He returned to the guest room and found Simone still there on the floor, kneeling like he'd ordered. He walked around her, studying her face. Her eyes were lowered again and the expression she wore was one of complete peace. No fear. Not even nervousness. Her confidence gave him confidence.

He pulled off his t-shirt and dropped it on the floor.

Jason extended the crop and put the leather flapper under her chin, lifting it. He'd done that a thousand times in a thousand fantasies but this was the first time he'd ever done it to a real person in real life. His head swam. He swallowed hard before he could speak.

"You're a good little slave," he said softly.

"Thank you, sir," she whispered.

"I haven't kissed you yet. I keep thinking I ought to do that."

"My body's yours, sir," she said. "Every part of it."

"Do you want me to kiss you?" he asked.

"I want what you want, sir."

"I want you to tell me if you want me to kiss you."

"Yes, sir. I would love it if you kissed me."

"If you're a good girl for me, maybe you'll earn a kiss or two."

He'd said that a thousand times in his fantasies. *Earn it. Do it. Obey me. Lay there. Spread for me. Take it. Take all of it...*

But even in his wildest fantasies he never dreamed he'd meet a girl who wanted to hear those words as much as he wanted to say them.

He lowered the crop to his side and stepped forward, right in front of her.

"Take my cock out," he said to her, another line from a thousand fantasies. "Suck it."

She didn't hesitate one second before lifting her hands to unbutton his jeans, to push the denim open and aside to get to him. She wrapped both her small hands around him as she brought the tip to her lips.

"Take it," he said. "Right now. Every inch."

She obliged him with a smile, drawing his cock into her mouth, into her throat. The wet heat of her tongue was heaven. He hadn't had sex in a couple months, and the most recent time had been awkward and disappointing for the both of them. But this was everything he'd wanted for as long as he could remember wanting this. Jason slipped the crop's strap over his wrist and cupped the back of Simone's head in his hands. Gently he moved his hips, fucking her mouth as she sucked him and stroked him. Jason could barely contain himself as she pulled him into her mouth over and over again, rubbed him and pleasured him. Everything was so tight inside him. Every muscle was tense and every nerve vibrated. He could come at any moment.

"Slow down," he said softly and she let up on the intensity. "That's good. I'm going to come on you. When I tap you with the crop, you're going to sit back and open your shirt." She managed somehow to both nod in agreement and keep sucking him at the same time. God, she was good at this.

Jason took his crop in hand again. Now that he wasn't trying to hold off coming, he let himself gaze down at her, watch her. He committed the images to memory—her pink lips wrapped around his cock, her eyes closed in concentration, her bare feet against the rug, his hands twined in her soft hair. He looked up and caught a glimpse of them in the mirror that hung on the back of the door. Simone on her knees with his cock in her mouth and him standing, looming over her with a crop in his hand. Was that him? Really him? The sort of man who did this to women? Made one serve him sexually like a slave? Apparently so. The mirror didn't lie.

The pressure built so hard Jason had to close his eyes. A groan escaped his throat. His hips moved of their own accord. He needed to come. He'd die if he didn't. He struck the side of Simone's thigh with the crop and she immediately pulled back and with both hands untied the knot and let the shirt fall open. She had beautiful large breasts and red nipples. He came at the sight of them, at the sight of her arching her back, offering herself to him. With his cock in his hand, he came on her chest, on her breasts and stomach and neck in heady, hard spurts. Soft sounds escaped his lips. The pleasure was as intense as he'd ever felt it.

He could barely stand when he'd finished, he was so spent. With his crop he motioned for Simone to lie on the bed. She stretched out on her back and he straddled her hips. He gathered both of her wrists in one hand and pressed them over her head into the sheets. When she was pinned there, covered in his come, looking like every dream he'd ever had in his entire adult life, he finally kissed her.

———

THE STORY CONTINUES in Picture Perfect Cowboy, *available now in trade paperback, ebook, library hardcover, and audio from 8th Circle Press and Tantor Audio.*

A WELL-STOCKED DUNGEON

EXCERPT FROM "THE PRIEST," THE NINTH BOOK IN THE ORIGINAL SINNERS SERIES

When a New Orleans parish priest is found dead of an apparent suicide, the police see no reason to investigate. Private detective Cyrus Tremont knows a cover-up when he sees it, however. A former cop, he's seen it all...or so he thought.

Clues point him in the direction of Nora Sutherlin, an erotic romance writer who moonlights as a dominatrix. Together, they form an unlikely bond built on their shared need for justice.

In this excerpt, Nora reunites in New Orleans with her lover, Søren, after a long break....

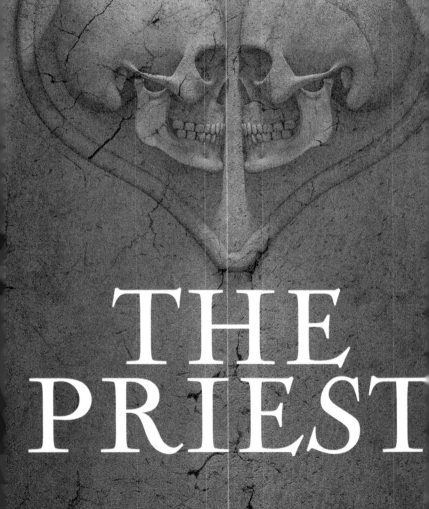

THE
PRIEST

Nora watched Søren as he opened the drawers of her curio cabinet, hunting for something very specific.

"What are you looking for?" she asked.

"I haven't decided yet. But not this."

Søren pulled a massive twelve-inch dildo out of a drawer and held it up. "Really, Eleanor?"

"That's not mine, I swear," she said. "I only use it on Sheridan."

Søren raised his eyebrow. "She's tiny."

"She's bigger on the inside. That's a Doctor Who joke."

"I went to school in England as I child. I fully understood the reference," he said as he put the gigantic dildo back in the drawer.

"My God, you have enough butt plugs to start a butt plug emporium," he said.

"You can never have too many butt plugs. If you're looking for the scalpels and knives, they're in the bottom drawer on the left."

"I wasn't…Or I thought I wasn't."

"I like that you can get an erection just by hearing the word 'scalpel.' It's like Pavlov's dog, except it's Pavlov's erection."

"Don't mention dogs if you want me to keep it."

Nora grinned sleepily. "You can slice me up if you want. I don't mind. You'll be hard until breakfast."

"Blood-play? On white sheets?"

"Hmm…good point. If they were cheap, I'd say go for it but this is Millesimo Egyptian cotton. Sheridan got them for me."

"We'll avoid bloodstains then," he said. He took from a drawer a long thin carbon fiber rod—a misery stick—and set it on the bedside table by the lamp.

Clearly Søren was in a mood to bring the pain.

"Did you really not beat and fuck King tonight?"

"I did not. After last night, he'll be needing more than a day to recover," Søren said with a little sinister note of giddiness in his tone.

"Oh, great," Nora said. "Now I have an erection."

Søren lowered his head.

"What?" she asked.

He lifted his head. "Nothing. Except I'm glad you've decided you'll never leave me. Because even if I could live without you, I would never want to."

"You should kiss me after you say stuff like that."

"I will," he said. "But I'm going to torture you first. Adjustable spreader bar?"

"How short we talking?"

"Twelve to fourteen inches."

"There's a one-footer on the wall by the med table."

"Ankle cuffs?"

"In the cabinet over the sink."

"Stay put."

Søren—magnificently naked—strode from the little bedroom into her dungeon. Like she'd go anywhere with that view…

He returned quickly with all his little wicked implements —the spreader bar and the ankle cuffs.

And one leather strip, about a foot long and a couple inches wide. He must have cut it off her flogger with the thick fat tails.

"What's that for?" she asked as Søren passed her the leather strip.

"You may need to bite down on something," he said. "Turn over."

Just like that…all the sleepy two a.m. joking stopped. It stopped like someone had flipped a switch, turned off the lights, turned on the pain. He could do that, Søren, with a glance and a subtle change of tone that came with the standard warning—I am not playing anymore.

But neither was Nora.

She turned over as ordered and rested her cheek against the cool white sheets. Søren took each ankle in his hands and wrapped and buckled the cuffs around them. With small hooks, he secured the cuffs to the spreader bar.

Then he picked up the misery stick.

Then he grabbed the metal bar in the middle and pulled her into place as if she weighed nothing.

Then he lifted the bar, forcing her to bend her knees. Her feet were at his stomach on either side. Nora started breathing hard.

She had a very bad feeling about this.

"I'd bite down on the strap now if I were you," Søren said.

"You're going to beat the soles of my feet, aren't you?"

"Yes."

"Fuck." Nora grabbed the leather strap and put it between her teeth.

She hated foot torture.

Hated it.

Not the good kind of hate. Not the playful kind of hate. Not the "Oh no, not that, sir, anything but that, sir."

She would rather take a hundred cuts from a scalpel, an hour-long session with a single-tail whip, or even red-hot wax-play that left her covered in first degree burns. Foot torture was one of her limits.

But it wasn't a hard limit which meant she wouldn't safe out if Søren tried it.

No, she wouldn't safe out.

But she wasn't going to enjoy it.

She couldn't even enjoy Søren's thumbs on her insoles, caressing them tenderly. She was too tense, too scared, already breaking out into a cold sweat.

"You broke someone's foot tonight," he said. Nora didn't say the kid deserved it. Søren knew that.

He just didn't care. If he could use it as an excuse to push her to the edge of her pain threshold, he would use it.

On nights like this…she hated him as much as she loved him.

"There is no one in the world that respects your sadistic impulses more than I," he continued, "but I would be very disappointed if you got yourself arrested or sued. One of these days, Eleanor, you really are going to have to learn to control that temper of yours."

He caressed her ankles, all those delicate little bones. She wanted to cry. Instead she grabbed a pillow and shoved her under her breasts. It would help to have something to cling to during…

"Only five, I promise." He ran his fingertips gently over the tops of her feet.

Five.

She could take five. She could survive that.

"On each foot."

Nora whimpered. Not as a joke. Not being playful. Not to get his sympathy. Not trying to be funny.

She whimpered because she was scared.

And she knew he knew that.

But he picked up the misery stick anyway.

The thing about misery sticks, Nora knew from experience, was that they were deceptive little toys. They didn't look like they could hurt much. Nothing but very long, very thin metal rods. That's it.

Except when you pulled the tip of the rod back and let it go, flicking it against the bare skin, it hurt worse than being sliced open by a knife that had been sitting in a red-hot fire.

And she was about to take five strikes on each foot.

The metal spreader bar rested across Søren's stomach.

She could flinch and twist but there would be no getting away from him.

"Shall we get this over with?" he asked.

Nora nodded her head quickly. The sooner the better. The building anticipation was only adding to her misery.

They were called misery sticks for a reason, after all.

"Left foot or right first?" he asked. Nora shrugged. "I wasn't asking you. Only talking to myself."

His tone was taunting. Sometimes when he got like this, she could almost believe he hated her a little, too. But she knew better. As cruel as he could seem when he was hurting her, she knew it was a kind of love. Søren's sadism was as much a part of him as his faith and his love and his mercy. That he could be like this with her without fear meant he loved her enough not to hide this side of himself from her.

She told herself that as he picked up the misery stick off the table.

"Feet flexed," he said. "Both of them. No curling the toes or I'll make it ten."

Nora had to fight every instinct in her body to flex her feet. A hot tear ran from her eyes and down onto the Millesimo Egyptian cotton sheets.

Her entire body was tense as a violin bowstring.

And Søren plucked it.

One.

He flicked the misery stick once and the strike landed at the back of her left heel.

Nora flinched. She couldn't help it. Flinched and whimpered again as her teeth dug deep into the leather strap in her mouth.

Two.

He flicked it again, half an inch down the heel, inching closer and closer to the sensitive arch.

Three.

The arch was next. She knew it. She braced herself and wasn't surprised when the next thing she felt was nearly the worst physical agony in her life.

She screamed into the pillow.

"I shouldn't enjoy it so much when you're in this kind of pain," he confessed. "But I do."

Four.

He struck her again, even higher, closer to the toes.

Nora's head swam. She thought for a second she might actually pass out.

"Flex, Eleanor. Flex."

She couldn't. She was in so much pain, she couldn't make herself flex her foot.

"Oh, fine," he said. "I'll do it myself."

He took her toes in his hands, and pushed, forcing her foot to flex.

"Now keep it there," he ordered.

She did.

Five.

He hit the ball of her foot.

"Five," he said. "Now that wasn't so bad, was it?"

He set the stick down on the table again and Nora shuddered. She shuddered because he'd started rubbing her foot, tenderly stroking all the burning places.

"I know you hate this," he said softly. "And deep down, there is a small part of me that hates myself for how much I enjoy it. Sometimes I wish it didn't have to be like this. You understand?"

With the leather strap still clenched between her teeth, Nora could only nod, so she did.

"But," Søren said, "it is like this. And we have five more to go."

He picked up the misery stick again.

The last five hurt as badly as the first five, but she took

them better, mostly because she was nearly out of her mind with pain. At five, she went limp, as limp as a rag doll or a corpse. She barely felt it when Søren unhooked the spreader bar, hardly noticed when he removed the leather strap from her mouth.

"You nearly bit through it," he said. He sounded impressed.

Nora rolled into the fetal position, toes curled, feet aching.

Søren pulled her to him and held her back against his chest.

"You can cry if you need to." He spoke softly into her ear as he ran his fingers through her sweat-damp hair.

"I hate that so much," she said, a small sob escaping her throat.

"I know, Little One. I know you do." He slid over her, on top of her and positioned her under him. He was so aroused, she felt the tip of his erection against her stomach, throbbing like it wanted to force its way into her, any way it could.

He kneed her thighs open and she was too weak to stop him, even if she wanted to.

"That was almost too much for you, wasn't it?" he asked. She nodded again. He smiled. "My brave little girl," he said and kissed her forehead.

Søren braced himself over her and through watering eyes she saw him lick two fingertips and then press those same fingers against her vulva. He pushed through her folds and into her vagina. She yielded to him easily, her body offering no resistance.

"And this is why I would never let you leave me," he said. "You hated that with every fiber of your being…and you're dripping wet."

She was still crying when he entered her, splitting her.

His thick cock went deep on the very first stroke. She cried out again, in pleasure this time, not pain.

Sometimes she hated herself, too.

But not very much.

Søren found her mouth and kissed her, his cock slipping ever deeper into her as they kissed. Since her feet hurt so much every time they brushed the sheets, she wrapped her legs around Søren's lower back as he thrust into her. They fucked in a frenzy, and the need was as much as hers as his. His hands dug into the tender flesh of her breasts as he held them, squeezing them as he rode her.

It wasn't enough to let him have her. She had to have him in return. Nora clung to his shoulders and with her legs twined around him, she lifted her hips again and against to him, taking his cock as hard as he gave it to her. The pain wasn't the thing. She wasn't aroused by having her toes stepped on by a stranger in a crowd any more than she was aroused by the strike of a metal bar on her insoles. It was him, Søren, and who he turned into when he let himself free with her. The master. The monster. The beautiful sadist. That was the secret she never told anyone, not even herself, that she loved him more for his cruelties than his mercies. He was kind to everyone he met.

He was only cruel to his lovers.

Pavlov's cruelty.

Søren hadn't bound her wrists so she was free to pass on a little cruelty of her own. She slid her hands down his long back and every time his cock made her vagina spasm, she dug her fingernails into his skin. He let her do it—but only twice.

Then he pulled out and turned her onto her hands and knees. Søren forced her legs wider from behind, so wide her belly touched the bed. He entered her with a rough thrust, impaling her hard enough she cried out. But his fingertips found her clitoris and stroked it as he used her from behind, stroked her until she was nearly blind with the need to come.

Søren gripped her by her shoulders, thumbs on the back of her neck, immobilizing her against the bed.

His thrusts seemed endless but so did her desire for them. Long moans escaped her lips that she stifled as best she could in the sheets. Søren's fingers knew her body too well. He had her trapped at the edge of orgasm but wouldn't let her fall over yet. He held her there with his touch and the organ that pinned her place as it slid in and out of her slick hole. He might punish her if she came without permission.

She came anyway. She couldn't help it or stop it. She was too wet and the fingers stroking her were too wet and everything inside her quivered and tensed and there was no telling her body no when it was ready to scream yes.

When she came, she buried her mouth against the bed to scream and only the last syllable of it hit the air as Søren lifted her bodily back against him. She sunk down on his cock as he held her on his knees. His hand came around and clasped her throat. His mouth was at her ear so she could his ragged breaths. He fucked up and into her until his own release. He inhaled and inhaled, his breath hitching and she knew he was coming inside her, filling her with semen and she craved it.

Only when he finished with her, did he release his iron grip on her throat. He let her go and she nearly collapsed onto the bed. Søren lay down on his back next to her, ran one hand through sweat-soaked hair and then used his hand as a pillow.

"You'll have to apologize to Sheridan about the sheets," he said.

"What? It's okay. Come comes out."

"Blood might not."

"Blood?"

"I should have just cut you up," he said, laughing softly.

"Did you make me bleed?" she asked, holding her foot out, studying it for wounds.

Søren rolled onto his side away from her.

He had eight bleeding claw marks on his back just under his shoulder blades.

"Fuck," Nora said, then laughed. "Oops?"

⸺

THE STORY CONTINUES in The Priest, *available now in trade paperback, ebook, library hardcover, and audio from 8th Circle Press and Tantor Audio.*

THE TEACHER'S PET

THE COMPLETE SHORT STORY FROM THE "FELT TIPS" ANTHOLOGY

Shoshanna Evers, Kelly Jamieson, Karen Stivali, Karen Booth, and forty other authors shared their office-supply-inspired fantasies in Felt Tips: Office-Supply Erotica, *an eclectic anthology of erotic literature published by 8th Circle Press (now long out of print, unfortunately). This collection was edited by Tiffany Reisz, who contributed "Teacher's Pet," an exclusive Original Sinners short story featuring Mistress Nora and her client Sheridan. The story is presented here in its entirety.*

FELT TIPS

One of these days Sheridan would learn that Mistress Nora heard everything. Memory of an elephant and one little random stray sentence uttered in her presence was as eternal as a topless photo posted on the Internet. She remembered the night she made the off-hand comment about teachers being among the various authority figures she'd always found attractive. She'd been at Kingsley's for a party--not as a guest but as a servant. Nora, Kingsley, Griffin were all there along with a few of the more highly-favored submissives who'd been given the honor of serving the Dominants their dinner and wine.

"I don't remember ever having crushes on my teachers," Mistress Nora had said as she drained the last of her red wine. She snapped her fingers in Sheridan's direction, and Sheridan returned to the Mistress's side with the bottle. "Not in high school anyway. I only had eyes for You-Know-Who."

Kingsley gave her a lascivious knowing grin.

"You-Know-Who was a teacher when he was eighteen. Taught modern languages at our school," Kingsley reminded Nora after he too had finished his wine. She loved being around Kingsley when he'd had more than a glass. His French accent grew thicker, his hands wandered even more. "I used to stand outside his classroom and watch him. I'd never seen such alert students."

"They must have been terrified of him, Monsieur," Sheridan said as she poured for the Mistress. She stiffened slightly when she felt a hand on the back of her knee. She'd put on a little white cocktail dress, white strappy heels and no panties whatsoever before coming to serve at Kingsley's table. The white dress Mistress Nora had picked out. The total lack of underwear? That had been Sheridan's idea.

"*Non, pas du tout,*" Kingsley said, leaning forward and steepling his fingers. "They adored that blond monster. Absolute devotion."

"I know that feeling," Mistress Nora said as she slid her hand up Sheridan's thigh. Sheridan put a hand on the table to steady herself as the Mistress slipped one finger into her. "I hated school until him. But once I had him helping me with my math homework...let's just say homework became a far pleasanter experience."

"I always helped him grade the French homework." Kingsley took a ripe red grape from a silver bowl and popped it into his mouth. "One red pencil and I could bleed all over those poor boys' papers. It's an *accent aigu*, not rocket science."

And that's when Sheridan had said it, rather under her breath and entirely off-hand: "I wish one my teachers had fucked me when I was in high school. That would have been so hot...illegal, but so hot."

But she couldn't be held accountable for a statement like that, could she? Not with Nora's index finger tickling her cervix.

Mistress Nora hadn't said a word about it that night, about Sheridan's long-ago dream to be sexually used by one of her teachers. The conversation had moved on to other, safer subjects than the man Mistress Nora called You-Know-Who and Kingsley called The Blond Monster. That had been over a month ago...six weeks even. So it never occurred to Sheridan that one day she'd call to make an appointment with the Mistress and receive this as an answer

"Little Miss, I think we need to explore your erotic fascination with authority figures, authority figures other than powerful men in business suits. Dress like a school girl and wait in Kingsley's playroom. Wear panties this time. That's an order."

Nora hung up before Sheridan could even utter her usual, "Yes, Mistress."

Sheridan had gone to a public high school in Chicago and

hadn't worn uniforms, but she knew the Mistress had gone to parochial schools all her life. Something about that Catholic schoolgirl uniform just did it for Sheridan. Hopefully it would do it for the Mistress too.

She gave herself a once-over in the mirror in one of Kingsley's bedrooms. She'd found a red and black pleated skirt and pulled it on and some white cotton panties. They seemed rather safe and schoolgirl-esque. A white polo shirt to match her white knee socks and saddle shoes completed her transformation. She'd arranged her blond hair into pigtails with little white bows. At twenty-three, Sheridan still had small, pert breasts, so she didn't even bother with a bra. The Mistress had demanded panties. No other underwear had been mentioned.

As she looked at herself in the mirror, Sheridan felt the first rush of arousal. She loved scening with the Mistress. Why more women didn't play with a Dominatrix was beyond her. As one of Mistress Nora's very few female clients, Sheridan knew she occupied a rather privileged position. The men who came to the Mistress paid through the nose to get brutalized and beaten into a bloody pulp by the legendarily sadistic Dominatrix. Sheridan got the beatings too, but she got one thing the men didn't get--orgasms handdelivered by the infamous Little Red Riding Crop herself.

By the time Sheridan got to the playroom, she knew she was already starting to soak her white cotton panties. No one had the power to get her off quite like The Mistress. Nora knew all Sheridan's secret fetishes--business suits, powerful authority figures, being treated like a little girl who existed solely to be used for another person's sexual pleasure...

Sheridan opened the door to Kingsley's playroom and nearly laughed out loud. It had been transformed from a BDSM dungeon, albeit a posh one, into a classroom--large rolling chalkboard and desk included. An old-fashioned student's desk sat at the middle of the room in front of the chalkboard. She did laugh out loud at what the Mistress had written on the board--"Ms. Sutherlin." Apparently she wasn't to call her Mistress Nora today. Ms. Sutherlin...she could get used to that.

Sheridan took her seat at the desk and waited. She wasn't sure how much time passed--five minutes, maybe ten. But it seemed like an hour of breathless impatience waiting for the Mistress to arrive. When the door opened behind her, Sheridan held her breath.

"Well, at least you're on time for class today," came a woman's voice from over her shoulder, cold and stern. "You missed yesterday."

"I'm sorry, Ms. Sutherlin. I didn't mean to miss class." Sheridan tried to sound as contrite as possible, and it came out sounding genuinely repentant. During her BDSM sessions with the Mistress, Sheridan put all her years of stage training to good use.

"You didn't just miss class, Young Lady," Nora said, coming to stand in front of Sheridan. "You missed a test."

Sheridan looked up at Nora and nearly broke character with a smile. Usually Nora dressed in men's style business suits for their sessions. Sheridan had such a fetish for Armani that merely being around a man or woman in such a suit could get her halfway to orgasm. But today the beautiful black-haired, green-eyed Dominatrix had gone all out to play the part of the stern and scary teacher. She wore a tight black pencil skirt, a white blouse tucked in, and black and white heeled spectator shoes. Her beautiful wavy black hair was pulled back into a severe bun, and she had on black retro-chic glasses. As if she didn't look powerful and erotic enough, she even wore a black tie with a perfect Windsor knot at her neck. There wasn't a straight high school boy in the world who wouldn't drop to his knees in front of Ms. Sutherlin and pledge his eternal devotion. Sheridan certainly would.

"A test? I forgot about the test." Sheridan laid her head down on her desk in absolute defeat.

"Yes, a test. You have a zero where a grade should be. Now what should we do about that, young lady? Leave it a zero?"

"I can do make-up work," Sheridan said, raising her head and looking up at Nora. "I'll do anything. A paper, a make-up test...anything."

"Anything?"

Sheridan nodded eagerly. "Absolutely anything. I have to get into a good college," she said, almost laughing again. All her young life her father had drilled the importance of getting good grades into her. Good grades, good college, good life. Instead of college, she'd gone to Broadway, become an actress, and now made six-figures an episode on her TV show. But playing submissive to Mistress Nora...that was her favorite role.

"I'm sure we can come up with some make-up work you could do for me," Nora said as she came to stand behind Sheridan's desk. She gently tugged on one of Sheridan's curling blond pigtails.

"I'm sure we could too, Ms. Sutherlin."

As the Mistress stroked her hair, Sheridan closed her eyes and reveled in the touch of the two hands that knew her body as well as she knew her own. She'd played with Nora for a couple of years now, having sessions whenever the stress of the real world got to be too much for her. Lately that translated to almost every week. Nora--Ms. Sutherlin today--ran her fingers over the back of Sheridan's neck before slipping her hand down the front of Sheridan's shirt.

Sheridan gasped as Nora lightly plucked her left nipple.

During their first session together, Nora had given Sheridan ample warning before every touch, every intimacy. Now as they'd played together so much, Nora knew exactly how to touch her. The more intrusive and possessive Nora was with her body, the more Sheridan liked it. For a few long and wonderful minutes, Nora did nothing but caress Sheridan's breasts, teasing her nipples, bringing them to pert attention. Sheridan sat as still as she could, clinging hard to her chair as Nora dug inside her shirt.

Without warning Nora pulled her hand out of Sheridan's collar and slapped the desk hard.

"Chalkboard. Now." Sheridan stood up and nearly ran to the board. "Write 'I will not miss a test ever again.'"

Sheridan picked up the chalk and began to write the words as instructed. But her handwriting quickly deteriorated as Nora pressed her body into Sheridan's back and lifted her shirt over Sheridan's breasts.

"Keep writing," Nora whispered in her ear. "I didn't say you could stop."

"Yes, Ms. Sutherlin." Sheridan swallowed as she tried to focus on the words. It wasn't easy ignoring the pleasant things her teacher was doing to her bared breasts. Nora nipped at Sheridan's ear and dropped a deep kiss onto her neck. In real life, Sheridan never found herself attracted to women. But Mistress Nora was no ordinary woman. The Dominatrix had twice the confidence and power of any man she'd ever met. Plus Sheridan was never expected to do anything to Nora in return. A Dominatrix's body was off-limits to clients apart from the occasional kiss on the boot. Sheridan could relax completely with Nora and be touched, used, and fucked without any pressure to recipro-cate. She lived with constant demands from directors, publicists, producers, agents, and the press. An hour of Nora's time cost her four figures but she considered it worth every penny. She wasn't buying sex. She was buying sanity.

"I know you weren't sick yesterday," Nora said, kneading both of Sheridan's breasts at once. Sheridan moaned in the back of her throat. "I know you were just playing hooky. And we both know you'll have to be punished for that."

"Punished?" Sheridan's voice quivered as she kept writing.

Nora pulled away from Sheridan, and she heard a desk drawer opening and closing. Then Nora was at Sheridan's back again, but this time she pressed a hand into Sheridan's throat.

"Punished," Nora rasped into her ear. Sheridan looked down and watched as Nora pinched her nipple, then brought up a small black binder clip and clamped it onto the soft pink bud. Sheridan flinched, the slight pain sending a thrill like an electric current straight to her clitoris. "Severely punished." Nora clamped her other nipple with a second binder clip.

Sheridan dropped the chalk as Nora grabbed her by the back of the neck, spun her toward the desk, and pushed her over. The drawer squeaked as Nora once again opened it. Sheridan didn't even look to see what Nora had pulled out. She wasn't sure she wanted to know.

"It was a math test you missed yesterday. Let's see if you can even count, Little Miss. Count by sevens for me. Don't get one wrong."

Something hit the back of Sheridan's thighs, something long and hard and thin.

"Seven," Sheridan said.

Another strike in the same spot and Sheridan gasped from pain.

"Fourteen."

A third blow hit a little lower...twenty-one...a fifth landed at the very top of her thighs, thirty-five...by seventy-seven,

Sheridan's thighs were on fire. Nora dropped her implement of torture on the floor and Sheridan saw what she'd been beaten with--a wooden yard stick.

"Good girl. Didn't miss a single one."

"Thank you, Ms. Sutherlin."

"You really are a very good student even if you did miss a test yesterday. I think you'll ace the make-up examination."

"Examination?" Sheridan repeated, the word giving her a shiver of excitement. "I think I'm ready for an exam."

"Let's find out."

Nora pulled the desk chair out and took her seat in it right behind Sheridan. She flipped Sheridan's skirt up onto her back and pulled her panties all the way down and off Sheridan's legs. With her high-heeled feet, Nora pushed Sheridan's legs wide open.

With both hands, Nora began to examine Sheridan. She rubbed Sheridan's already swollen clitoris while her fingers probed deep inside her body. Sheridan went limp against the wooden desk as Nora opened her wider and wider and delved deeper and deeper into her.

Nora never rushed this part of their scene. She knew Sheridan loved it too much, needed it too much. When men looked at a vagina, they only thought about how quickly they could stick their cock inside it. But Nora treated Sheridan's genitals like a mystery that needed methodical study to solve.

With the pads of two fingers, Nora made tight, intense circles into Sheridan's g-spot. The noises that escaped Sheridan's lips were of the animal variety. Her nipples ached from the clips, her vagina growing wetter and hungrier with each passing second. She needed release so terribly she was almost ready to beg for it.

Only the discipline Nora had instilled in her kept Sheridan from pleading for more. The release would come in time. She had to be patient for it and let the Mistress have her delicious way with her.

Sheridan's vaginal muscles contracted as Nora dug both thumbs into her and pulled her open wider.

"I think you'll pass this exam, Little Miss," Nora said. "I can see right inside you."

Sheridan rested her forehead on the desk with a desperate groan. Nora pulled her hands out of Sheridan, gave her a viciously hard slap on the bottom, before standing up again.

"Up," she ordered. Sheridan slowly stood, almost dizzy from desire. "Sit on the desk. Lay on your back."

Sheridan didn't hesitate before complying. On her back was easily her favorite place to be, especially around her Mistress.

Nora removed the first binder clip and caressed her sore nipple. The pleasure of the massage made the momentary pain more than worth it. The pain threw the pleasure into such stark relief that sex without pain these days almost always meant sex without pleasure as well. Nora removed the other binder clip.

"Better?"

"Thank you, Ms. Sutherlin." Sheridan smiled in bliss. She thanked the Mistress every chance she had--thanked her for the punishment she deserved, thanked her for the release from it.

"Don't thank me quite yet..." Nora reached back into the desk drawer and pulled out a clear plastic ruler. "Open wide for me."

In any other setting, Sheridan would have taken that as an order to open her mouth. But with Nora, it meant to open her legs. Nora sat on the desk next to her hips, and pulled Sheridan's left leg over her thighs. With the flat of the ruler, she dropped short sharp slaps onto Sheridan's vulva and clitoris. Sheridan flinched and gasped at the combination of pain and pleasure all in one. Blood rushed to her hips and it took everything she had not to close her thighs.

The assault ended quickly and Sheridan could only pant for air as Nora dropped the ruler and began to finger her again.

"You're wet, Little Miss," Nora said. "I think I could fit my whole arm in you if I tried."

"Please..." Sheridan had given up all her dignity by this point. "I need to come, Ms. Sutherlin."

"I can tell. Can you?"

Sheridan raised her head and watched as Nora spread the wet lips open. She could see the wetness on Nora's fingers, see her own swollen clitoris.

"Yes, Ms. Sutherlin."

Once more the desk drawer opened and this time Nora pulled out a tube of lubricant and an impressively-sized vibrator. Nora had dozens of different sex toys that she used on Sheridan during their sessions, but the larger phallic vibrators were some of Sheridan's favorites. Her orgasms were always stronger during penetration but she could almost never orgasm during normal penetrative sex. Not with vanilla men anyway. They had no idea what to do with a girl like her. But Nora knew...oh, Nora knew everything...

Nora applied the lubricant to Sheridan with quick efficiency. The cold liquid soothed the burning but not the ache for orgasm.

Nora turned the vibrator onto a slow setting and slowly eased it into Sheridan. Her inner muscles gripped at it hungrily as it moved in deeper. Slowly in and quickly out She breathed, focusing only on the ceiling, on relaxing her whole body to take the toy all the way into her. With one hand Nora wielded the vibrator and with her other she played with Sheridan's clitoris, rubbing it in tight circles while her whole body trembled from the inside out. The entire world fell away as Sheridan plummeted into subspace. She was nothing now, nothing but a body, a hole, an object to be used for another's pleasure. She had no heart, no soul, no ego, no personality. She was nothing but the tightening inside her, the coiling of pleasure, the deep internal throbbing...the need, the all-consuming need...

Sheridan's back arched off the table as she orgasmed so hard her muscles almost expelled the vibrator from her vagina. But Nora held it in as wave after wave of ecstasy racked her entire body. A second orgasm came hard on the heels of the first. She cried out, nearly in pain from the flood of sensations washing over her. Nora wouldn't let her give up or give in.

"One more, Little Miss...just one more..."

Sheridan gripped the edge of the desk as Nora brought her to climax a third time. Her head came off the wood and her stomach muscles rippled from the powerful contractions that slammed into her. Finally Nora pulled the vibrator out of her and let Sheridan merely rest on the desk, her eyes closed, the world still a thousand miles away.

Somewhere in the back of her mind, Sheridan tried to see herself laying on the desk, her white shirt bunched up around her neck, her breasts bared, her skirt around her stomach, her thighs open and her naked body open to anyone who wanted to see her.

She'd never felt so peaceful.

"Lie still," Nora ordered as she used a wet cloth to wipe the lubricant off Sheridan's wet folds. She loved this moment above all other. Even more than the orgasms, she loved when Nora took care of her afterwards with the tenderness of a mother. She'd always check her body for damage, for blood or tearing, for broken skin from the beating. Sheridan could clean herself up, of course, but it was the pinnacle of submission to let another person tend to her most personal needs. Sometimes after their longer sessions, Nora would even give her a bath, and wash every inch of her inside and out.

Nora cupped the back of Sheridan's neck and helped her come up off the desk to a sitting position. She pulled a bottle of water from the desk drawer, twisted the cap off, and let Sheridan drink while Nora pulled her shirt and skirt back into place, then slipped her panties back on her.

"Did I pass the test, Ms. Sutherlin?" she asked as Nora rubbed her lower back even as the last waves of orgasm dissipated. She felt utterly spent, completely emptied and entirely satisfied.

"Little Miss," Nora said, giving Sheridan one soft and forbidden kiss, "you not only passed the test, you are officially the teacher's pet."

ABOUT THE AUTHOR

Tiffany Reisz is the *USA Today* bestselling author of the Romance Writers of America RITA®-winning Original Sinners series from Harlequin's Mira Books.

Her erotic fantasy *The Red*—the first entry in the Godwicks series, self-published under the banner 8th Circle Press—was named an NPR Best Book of the Year and a Goodreads Best Romance of the Month.

Tiffany lives in Kentucky with her husband, author Andrew Shaffer, and two cats. The cats are not writers.

Subscribe to the Tiffany Reisz email newsletter:

www.tiffanyreisz.com/mailing-list

Printed in Great Britain
by Amazon